– 3 –

YASEMIN'S REVENGE

One voice among thousands

Nurgül Sönmez

Bibliografische Information der Deutschen Nationalbibliothek: Die Deutsche Nationalbibliothek verzeichnet diese Publikation in der Deutschen Nationalbibliografie; detaillierte bibliografische Daten sind im Internet über http://dnb.dnb.de abrufbar.

Die automatisierte Analyse des Werkes, um daraus Informationen insbesondere über Muster, Trends und Korrelationen gemäß §44b UrhG (Text und Data Mining") zu gewinnen, ist untersagt.

© 2021 Nurgül Sönmez

Lektorat: Berna Arslan
Korrektorat: Ömer Faruk Arslan - Arzu Kaya
Weitere Mitwirkende: Gamze Taşdemir

Verlag: BoD · Books on Demand GmbH, Überseering 33, 22297 Hamburg,
bod@bod.de
Druck: Libri Plureos GmbH, Friedensallee 273, 22763 Hamburg

ISBN: 978-3-7693-0880-8

Imprint

YASEMIN'S REVENGE – 3

Originally translated from German, published in 2022 ©

Nurgül Sönmez

Translation: Nurgül Sönmez
Compilation / Editor: Berna Arslan
Proofreading : Ömer Faruk Arslan
Final Check : Arzu Kaya
Book Cover Design: Gamze Taşdemir
Illustration / Index: Gamze Taşdemir

Author Contact Information:

✉ ns.nurgulsonmez@gmail.com

🅕 nurgulsonmez

📷 nurgulsonmezofficial

Team:

g.tsdmrr@gmail.com

To all book lovers...

Biography

Nurgül Sönmez

21.08.1979
Germany

In the years between 1995-2020, she often received awards.
She began writing in 1995 and has written countless poems,
song lyrics and novels. Written based on true events.
The rights to over 50 novels and over 2500 song lyrics were taken over
by various publishers and famous composers.
Now she no longer stands behind the scenes,
but with her works in the middle of the stage.

Nurgül Sönmez
– Schriftstellerin –

AUTHOR'S WORKS

- Her first book ANA (Poem - Turkish) was published in **2014**
- **2015** YASEMİN'İN SAVAŞI (Turkish)
- **2017** YASEMİN'İN İNTİKAMI (Turkish)

2021

- Matilda (Turkish, German)
- 1001 GECE YERİNE - BİN BİR GÜN (Turkish)
- STATT 1001 NACHT - TAUSENDUNDEIN TAG (German)
- YASEMİN'İN ÇARESİZLİĞİ 1 (Turkish)
- YASEMİN'İN SAVAŞI 2 (Turkish)
- YASEMİN'İN İNTİKAMI 3 (Turkish)

2022

- Matilda (English)
- YASEMINS VERZWEIFELUNG 1 (German)
- MAAROUF (Turkish, German)
- INSTEAD OF 1001 NIGHT - THOUSAND AND ONE DAY (English)
- YASEMINS KAMPF 2 (German)

2023

- YASEMINS RACHE 3 (German)

2024

- YASEMIN'S DESPERATION 1 (English)
- YASEMIN'S STRUGGLE 2 (English)
- YASEMIN'S REVENGE 3 (English)
- MAAROUF (English)

All books have been translated into French and are planned for future book projects. This will be followed by translations into Arabic and Spanish. If there is interest and demand, there will also be translation in other languages.

Her works © are based on true events and she continue to support social projects with the proceeds of the books.

Soon also available as audiobooks!

Nurgül Sönmez
– Schriftstellerin –

Thousands of voices can be hope for a voice.

Based on a true story!

Revenge!

The only thing keeping Yasemin alive. Everyone who caused this will feel the anger and pain of the last few years in the deepest depths.

No matter how much time has passed, Yasemin has not forgotten any of it.

Will the truth and justice prevail? Will Yasemin, now a successful businesswoman, be able to answer for all this?

The last episode of Yasemin and her siblings. All questions will be answered and the path to peace will be illuminated, closed doors will open. Perseverance, strength, success and patience will be rewarded...

Yasemin's Revenge

When Yasemin confronted her inner world and the negativities she had experienced during her struggle through the audio recordings, feelings of revenge came up in her unawares. I thought it was a momentary feeling, as if it would come and go. But it did come and eight years later it still hadn't gone away. I had heard it, seen it and understood it.

"Eight years." As Yasemin would go on to tell us, it had been eight years. So I began to wonder what Yasemin had recorded during that time. What developments and changes she had gone through in her life that I could later listen to on her audio recordings, which she had gradually sent to me, so I could turn the material into a book. My ability to write would depend on how Yasemin sent the cassettes.

She had given me her first cassette at our last meeting, which was a farewell, along with her recording assistant, so I could write the ending of my book Yasemin's Struggle. The further volumes came to my address by mail, with which I could start Yasemin's Revenge.

This time it should be different! Because I had no contact information of her. It was a bit of a strange feeling for me, not knowing where she was. The title of my next book would not be "YASEMIN'S STRUGGLE", but "YASEMIN'S REVENGE". I thought the title was very appropriate because she had always talked about revenge in her last recordings. But I didn't even know what kind of revenge it was. In fact, when I listened to the cassettes, I was frightened. Of course, I was afraid after such unpleasant events. What feelings did she have in her inner world that she chose revenge as her goal? What would her revenge look like? I was not aware of all this, and honestly, my hands were kind of tied.

If the question is awakened, why?

What kind of "REVENGE?", I wanted to find out while listening to her recordings. Had she gotten into a dangerous situation? "STOP YASEMIN!" I couldn't believe that or question it because I had no way to reach her to protect her from danger or to stop her from doing something stupid. Only she had my number, which was unfair to me. The balance was not right, I did not think her behavior was right.

And when the word "REVENGE" came up, how far was she going to go, when would she stop? "What if Yasemin confessed to a crime she had committed or was still planning?"

What should I do in such a situation? I think I will behave as I should. If Yasemin confessed to a crime she had committed, I had to do my human duty and report her, no matter how much I loved and respected her.

"Yasemin's Revenge!" gave me goosebumps.

Now; There is a huge difference between revenge and vengeance. I think you will agree with me.

While I was writing these lines, I had no idea what kind of revenge awaited us. Actually, it was an exciting task for me. After all these years, I had a huge question mark in my mind.

I had no choice but to wait, with each cassette she sent. Each time she loosened the blind knot a little, the question marks were solved one by one. But how long would this work take?

Exactly four days after our last meeting, I received the first cassette. Three weeks later, she sent the second one, which she had put in a large envelope. It was not the first cassette that I started with mixed feelings. What would Yasemin tell me about those eight years? What had she experienced? I was excited, looking forward to the cassettes.

CHAPTER
1

Why had I distanced myself from all my loved ones for eight years? Let's start from the beginning.

If you remember, after eight years, Nurgül and I had our first, but also last meeting, albeit briefly. It was very spontaneous, but the longing had been too great. It was very exciting for both of us.

Of course, we couldn't fit eight years into fifteen minutes the day we met, even if we had wanted to. The moment was too overwhelming, and we just looked at each other in the cafeteria as if frozen.

We were unconsciously focused on each other for seconds without saying anything.

And ... if you remember, after we said goodbye, I gave Nurgül an intake assistant and then we separated. She did not let me out of her sight until I was out of her sight. That moment was very meaningful to me. So, I had never stopped taking notes so that my feelings and thoughts would not be wasted. Although I had broken off communication for Nurgül's sake, I had still continued to record unintentionally.

"One day!", I said with longing.

Yes, one day! God willing, I was very eager to start all over again. I had been looking forward to this day, but we were not aware of the reunion. At some point, it had to happen again; I had prayed for that. There were exactly eight years between my first and last sound recording.

I had recorded deep themes. I wanted to send them to her one by one, I had a feeling that it had to be that way. But I still did not know why.

While sitting at the breakfast table with my siblings, it was important to make all decisions together.

Although it was not wanted, we came to an agreement:

"We must draw a line to our past in order to start our lives from scratch."

This time, we would direct our own lives. Others would no longer be allowed to determine our lives. A whole new life awaited us. It was a risky step, we were not aware of what we might encounter.

After some time I got used to taking new steps, because every time I had to take new steps in my life. Change was not difficult for me. Some people I knew said, "I could never start from scratch." So there were those who could and those who couldn't. Honestly I hadn't enjoyed starting from scratch with my siblings either, because I found myself in a difficult situation every time. There were moments when a person takes his power and strength from God alone, as God is our only refuge. Even though I did not like it, *how could one start from scratch every time to shake off such dangerous moments?*

I started a new life. I did not have the time or the strength, it happened on its own.

From now on, my notes were the first pages of a new life.

I had sent the first volume to Nurgül. She did not know that I would send it to her. At first, I was very curious, but I could imagine what had gone through her mind when she saw the cassette. Although she was one of my loved ones, I knew nothing about the developments in her personal life. Now it was time to see my loved ones.

"Finally, the time had come ..."

Nurgül and my other loved ones, whom I will talk about later, were not among those I wanted to take revenge on. They were people whom I loved and wanted to protect. Because I did not want to hurt them, my siblings and I had made a very serious decision at that time at the breakfast table.

Although this decision was very difficult for us, we had to carry it out. We were afraid of harming our loved ones, and although it was difficult, we had made this decision together.

It may be that I left eight years ago to protect my siblings and myself, even from the people I loved the most.

I was angry at myself for hurting my loved ones. For eight years, I could not overcome my anger. Maybe I still haven't managed to do so until today.

At that time, I could no longer stay in the state of North Rhine-Westphalia, so I moved to another state in Germany. This time, it was a metropolis ... It happened very quickly via the Internet. Within a day or two, I had gathered the job postings of almost twenty-five hairdressers. Wherever our destiny led, this new job would help us to answer one of the most important questions of our lives.

In which city would we live?

On the Internet, I searched for a hair salon, there I saw the pictures on their website, plus there were pictures of each employee. The pictures I saw were beautiful. There I wanted to go to work for a trial. So I said to myself, "Whatever happens, the hair salon opens at 7:30." After booking a hotel room, I packed a small bag for my needs and said goodbye to my siblings without wasting time, then I headed to the main train station.

This was the first experience we had as siblings. It was the first time we were separated from each other. The circumstances of life demanded it, it was a trial for each of us, even if only for one day and for one night.

While I packed my bag for my train ride, my siblings had prepared brioche rolls and snacks for dinner. My books that I wanted to finish reading and, of course, my admissions assistant would accompany me on the way.

Four and a half hours I would be traveling by train, to our unknown future. I was honestly excited, but this time the feeling was very different. We were going to decide where we were going. Not others would decide for us. We would not be forcibly or involuntarily subjected to a new situation. We would decide for ourselves. That had given me a very good feeling at the time. I remembered well that it increased my self-confidence, my head was clear, my gait was straight!

"The expected day" had come. In these lines you can now read what I had sent to Nurgül, how I had disappeared. I will continue where I had ended in the second book.

When you have no reason to stay,
you don't need a reason to go.

Yasemin's Struggle

CHAPTER
2

This time I really didn't know how and where to start talking. What if I said that I had a burden or stagnation? I was sorry that everything had turned out this way. I was tired and started my life all over again every time. *Didn't I have the right to build a normal and orderly life and live it like everyone else?* Until now, I had never been independent, never!

All decisions about our lives were made for us by others. No one cared what we wanted, even if it was against our will. We had to implement the decisions we made for us.

Just now, for the first time, I faced a situation with my siblings alone decision about our lives to make, this would not be easy for us. It was a difficult phase. A turning point where we had to break off contact with all our loved ones.

If it was just that, I would say ",Whatever", but my siblings and I would turn a whole new page. We were going to start from scratch in a new city. We would say "hello" to a brand new life, far away from everyone. We would leave without saying goodbye. My heart ached, it was too hard for me to say goodbye. Sometimes people have to implement the decisions they made in their lives, even if it was difficult and painful. But I felt compelled to implement the decision we made.

My destination was Hesse, I arranged to meet at the hair salon I had chosen through the job posting for a trial day from one of the ads.

On the train, I was recording the next shot. I had been on the road for about two and a half hours and still had an hour and a half ride ahead of me. I knew I had a long journey ahead of me, so I took my books that I had started and couldn't continue reading, my recording assistant, food and drink. On the train, I wanted to take advantage of the time. I had to change trains a total of three times, which cost me another hour.

Finally, my train ride was over. The hotel was right next to the hairdresser. After getting the keys at the reception, I retired to my room. I was in a metropolitan area... Everywhere was very crowded. Instinctively, I hoped I wouldn't *get lost here in the big city*. Anyway, then I said to myself, "Do your trial day first, the rest will come later."

For me, this long trip was actually like a rest day, like a regeneration. The weather was good, people flocked to the street to enjoy the sun. I couldn't see the hair salon from the window of my hotel room. Tomorrow morning I would have breakfast in the cafeteria just across the street so I could watch the hair salon while they were working.

Now, without wasting time, I wanted to visit the city a little. It was quite late. Everywhere the stores were closed, but still, I wanted to hurry a little. Although I was afraid of getting lost, I went determinedly.

It's **22:25**

Back in the hotel room, I was full. In my pajamas, I sat on my bed in rest mode. I leaned back comfortably while I continued my recordings, because I wanted to tell as much as possible.

In retrospect, of course, I was more mature today. I could certainly repeat this sentence years later, because experience makes a person mature. After all my experiences in my childhood years I had considered myself mature, but I was not. This I knew now.

Let's go back to the days when I was sold by my stepmother to a married man. The following questions went through my mind for a while. The gendarmerie had taken Uncle Ferhat away. But *where had they taken him? Where was he now? Had he only been arrested by the gendarmerie or was he also being punished? Would they ignore my complaint? These* questions gnawed at me. As these feelings and thoughts rose, I made a decision and began to investigate.

Immediately, I called the gendarmerie of our village, then I explained the situation to them. Although years had passed, the commander remembered that day. He looked up in the computer what had happened then. Within twenty-four hours, he had simply been released. This was expected, because I had not made a written complaint.

Why had this happened? He had touched me only one day. A year and a half after that he didn't, it was just that one day. *Why had he done that?* That one day inflicted deep wounds on me. After that, they had not left me alone, but tortured me day after day for a year and a half. This was not to go unpunished. I had called the police and asked what I should do. Then, as the police had told me, I had sent my complaint to the public prosecutor's office. While I had been living with my aunts in Germany, I had gathered all the necessary information. After I had submitted it, there had been radio silence for a long time, no letter or phone call. I had waited almost five months. When nothing came of it, I tried again to reach something by telephone, because I wanted to know the status of my written complaint. My Turkish residence seemed to be with the family that had adopted us, because they sent my letters there. Therefore, they could not process my complaint. However, I had given my address in Germany. Of course, there were some setbacks. My brother hadn't even noticed that there was a letter. It was as if they had completely cut us out of their lives, but I would still meet them. I was just waiting for that time.

Now we are in Yasemin's revenge! However, I had not mentioned many negatives in Yasemin's struggle. What I had mentioned so far was maybe twenty percent of what I had experienced. From the first day to the last, I was bullied, harassed, beaten, and tortured by everyone almost every day by my husband's family. It was difficult for me to accept this. Sometimes violence was not used, but instead various cruelties were committed. I was not allowed to go out for almost a year. I was officially held hostage in the house, I was like a prisoner, yet I was a child when I went through this. Something like that was not allowed to happen nowadays ... *Hadn't any of the neighbors seen it?*

Why hadn't they called the police to complain? What kind of world were we living in?

Forced detention is a crime!

While I was experiencing all of this, these questions gnawed at my mind, *"How can the criminal not be punished?"* These thoughts never left me. That is why I had devoted myself to this subject outside working hours.

Even after years, I wanted the criminals to be punished. Therefore, I would gradually take care of everyone who had hurt me back then. Individually, they would feel it. I was determined ...

The criminals had to be punished!

At that time I had been thirteen years old. I had been sold by my stepmother to a married man whom I had called uncle. When his wife could not have children, they had taken me to extend their generation. On the first day I was subjected to violence and a rape in a very horrible way. While I had lived through those nightmarish days, my experiences had a profound impact on my life. I was called names and pushed around every day. By every family member, by everyone. By everyone ...

About a year later I was finally allowed to enter the garden around the house. They tied a long iron chain to my foot. The other end was fixed in the concrete on the ground. Depending on which side of the garden I was working on, they lengthened or shortened the chain. But I could never go into the garden alone. Even though I was chained, there was always one or more with me. I was chained like a dog, it was a very bad feeling.

What had happened was truly an atrocity!

Days had come and gone. Yes, I do not hold on to those days. Only the deep wound in me had remained, it did not go away. This time had left deep scars on me. As if I were still bound to iron chains, these experiences tied me up. *What kind of tyranny was this? What kind of humanity was this?* My mind simply could not understand this cruelty. Fortunately, it was not enough, because I did not want to understand it either.

By now it is 11:45 pm, I finished my recording for today.

My interview and the trial work were over. Now I was on my way back by train, so I would like to continue my recordings as I had experienced the day.

Ready early in the morning I had woken up. After I had handed in the room key, I had watched the hair salon during breakfast. Already in the morning there was a rush of customers.

There were many customers, I had liked that. I had to be very convinced of my choice. Not only the employer should decide, I had to like and choose my new workplace. At first glance, everything was understandable. After my breakfast, I entered the salon just in time and introduced myself. Of course, I didn't know fluent German, as if I had been born and raised here. From my pronunciation it could be heard that I had come to Germany only later. After all, I had an accent. I accepted that, but it would get better with time, but I needed a little more time.

She liked the way I worked. After working in customer service for about two hours, she asked me to give her a wavy blow-dry hairstyle and then an updo. Her hair was nice and long and straight. I blow dried the waves the way she wanted, then did an elegant updo to her liking. She had liked it so much that she kept repeating that it was great. I was very talented at my craft. I knew I could do it because I was confident in what I was doing. There was an atmosphere of luxury in the salon. The look, the presentation, the quality, the professional products and the salon were great from start to finish.

Then I retreated to the back room with my new employer, that's where we had started talking. We had shaken hands, the only problem was moving there first. The co-worker she was working with was pregnant. She was leaving in three months when her notice period was up. That's why she was looking for a new employee.

In a luxurious hair salon, my salary would be more than at the jobs I had worked at until now. Of course, it was also a different state, the laws were different here. Hairdressers were paid more here. As we talked, she asked me for all sorts of seminar materials and my credentials. But I had neither, not even a completed apprenticeship. Yes, I had started the profession, but I had to give it up because I had moved. So I had been looking for a job as a clerk. Then she said to me, "If you can really do such beautiful updos and blow-dry like that, finish the apprenticeship you started here, but you'll get a normal hairdresser's salary from me. I need skilled hands like yours."

It had pleased me so much that she was so human. For my own future, of course, I would never refuse such an offer. So I had accepted it immediately.

"Now you will start in a luxury salon. You must do your hair beautifully, also be very well-groomed, already perfect, from the eyelashes to the nails," she admonished me kindly.

The hair salon where I was going to work was very elegant. There was no more crowding and quick check-in of customers. I had to keep up with my new luxurious job. In fact, I had to take care of my nails. *Working at home and gardening were not conducive.* True, I always used files, moisturizing creams and bright nail polish or even a bright clear polish. But I didn't go and get a manicure. The salon I had just worked at had cosmetic customer service. I was really excited! *Maybe this would change me, too. Maybe, as I entered a brand new life, I would say "hello" to a new Yasemin.*

What was life for a strange thing?

Already I was dreaming of the new life we would soon begin. It was another world for me. *Didn't I always have to start from scratch anyway? Hadn't I met a new life every time? Hadn't the new life I faced always made me stronger? Hadn't I matured through the wealth of experience? It had always been like that ... But didn't it also make life interesting that way?*

Colors of life;

It's not like watercolors, you can't keep the tone you want.

CHAPTER
3

I would like to briefly interrupt the cassette that Yasemin had sent me. So far we had listened to her, but from now on we will read her further story, what I have put together.

Yasemin was on the run so that she would no longer have to see and live the life she had experienced full of nightmares. Those who thought Yasemin had disappeared, I had to correct them, because I can say that Yasemin was right under their noses. So close to those who had hurt her. Even if they did not know it!

So far, Yasemin had expressed everything very well. This was a new life she would start, as an escape from being hurt again in her life. The new steps she would take from now on would make Yasemin a new person. What and which cassettes were waiting for me, I was really looking forward to. This was very exciting work for me, but I didn't even expect it to be like this.

The fact that she was hiding made the situation a little more exciting and gives this work a slightly different tension. Because I didn't know what was waiting for us. With the cassettes Yasemin sent me one by one, I didn't know what else she would tell me. As was evident from Yasemin's speeches, she was going through a period of drawing a line with the past. She was also able to move forward with her life very successfully.

I felt as if those eight years had never been an issue between us. As if time had been frozen. After all, we couldn't say that an existing problem existed. Because when I thought that Yasemin had stopped recording cassettes, in reality she had never stopped. What a great thing, I was surprised and full of joy.

Perhaps some of you had wondered, "Why didn't she publish this book eight years ago?" This was a fair question.

Why hadn't I published it? I was often asked this question in my private life. Normally, I had always answered like this:

"Before our story ended, Yasemin left!"

Therefore, I could not finish the end of Yasemin's real life tory. That was Yasemin's job. If I had written it myself and ended it with false facts, I would not have forgiven myself for it all my life. Because Yasemin's life was not my life. What if I had added or removed something myself. Would the right find its place then? It definitely wouldn't. Thinking this was Yasemin's job, I had neatly numbered her cassettes over the years and kept them in a special box. Some things really needed to be put together before they could come to an end. If you didn't swallow, you would choke. So now we take a deep breath and surrender to Yasemin's cassette again.

Blackened lives, written to be light, all books!

CHAPTER
4

When I continued my recordings, I never mentioned my siblings. We were in constant contact by phone. It was good for them and me. My sweet witch Kiraz had prepared food, they were waiting for me. I had nothing to worry about. Everything was as I had left it. They were very mature at that age. I was always grateful for that. They had not made my life difficult. I loved my two siblings very much. Both of them had been entrusted to me by God, and I felt that I had been commissioned by my Lord to take care of them. As if my two siblings were my test in this world. In order not to betray my Lord's trust and to finish my test properly, I had carried out my responsibility at a decent level and was still doing it.

Finally, I returned to the life I would end with good experiences and new perspectives. Now came the hour. My siblings were already asleep. But I had gone to the kitchen, lit the candles and wanted to talk to them a little.

I had talked about everything up to the last point with my siblings. My new employer said she would follow up on the apartment ads and help me find an apartment. I'm sure it was because we were from farther away. In other words, she had the approach that we would be in touch not only in business but also in our personal lives. Her caring had pleased me very much. She was a German, a very well-groomed woman;

blonde, tall and blue-eyed. She wore bright and sparkling diamond rings and necklaces, plus she smelled of perfume from head to toe.

Understandingly, my siblings said, "Sister, when you have seen it and decided, it will also be suitable for us." This, of course, had made my decision easier. In the same way, I imagined the new life we would build. I had beautiful dreams; I was immersed in a fantasy world. It was a pleasant feeling when I looked at our new life through the window of my imagination.

Before we moved, I had decided to get my driver's license. In such a short time, I had to increase my focus and spend every free minute learning. *Why shouldn't I have rushed it before?* After all, I knew this place, on the street I would have no problems, but in the big city we would move to, it would be difficult for me to get my driver's license.

Added to that was the task of finding a house and talking to my current place of employment. I had talked to the moving services beforehand to find out what was included in their services. This was very important to me.

Maybe I should buy some kitchen furniture for our new home. It should be a kitchen like in my dreams, like in the hair salon where I would start. It had very modern furniture, bright, purple and white in high gloss. There was an atmosphere with the employees like in an oasis of calm. Either way, I wanted a similar kitchen for our new house.

While I was going through such developments in my daily life, of course, I had never forgotten my deep scars, which were still reminders of my past. In the fatigue and hustle and bustle of the day, I spent my time, whenever I could, on our main topic. My revenge!

Happiness;
it's the best form of revenge!

Yasemin's Struggle

CHAPTER
5

Just now I was preparing my papers on the plane. Yes, you heard me right. Years later, I flew back to our homeland. I was very excited, but also very happy, because I had missed our country very much. But it would not be just a visit. There were all sorts of reasons for my departure, all of which I would explain one by one.

I felt that I had to gradually lay a foundation for myself in Türkiye. The sooner I started, the sooner it bore fruit. Therefore, it was time to tackle some issues that were important to me without further ado. All of them are punished one by one. First or last, sooner or later, every criminal is punished.

In the family that had adopted us, we had a nanny Aunt Meral and her husband, the gardener Uncle Osman. We had talked to them both on the phone, though not often. They would pick me up at the airport. Even today they were working for my brother, who was not to know of my coming. I wanted it that way.

To pick me up from the airport, Aunt Meral and Uncle Osman had been given leave. They had offered me to stay at their house in town. Therefore, I had not booked a hotel room. We had a lot to talk about and I knew they had my back. As soon as I arrived, I had to get serious without wasting time.

In order for my plan to succeed, I needed a few more people. I got their contact information from my uncle Osman. In my mind, I had already planned everything. As soon as I got off the plane, I would put it into practice. For this tiring time, I would spend two weeks in my country. For this I took my annual vacation. Everything was moving so fast that it was impossible to stop time.

By the way, my new employer had called me a few days ago. She had talked to her family and asked me to move into her mother's rental apartment in town. She mentioned that she could send me some pictures. The house was going to be huge with two stories and have a roof deck that was almost thirty square feet. She spoke so eloquently as if rental costs were between one thousand five hundred and two thousand euros. Maybe more, but that wasn't the case at all, because she had been talking to her mother. For some reason she talked to her about my situation. She told me that I was living with my siblings and so on and so forth, whatever she knew. Her mother also ran a hair salon. The customer area was for older people. The house was right above the hair salon. Almost six hundred euros had been deducted by her mother from her rent for the weekly cleaning of the hair salon and for me to work with her for a day, but her offers were still unfinished. If I had kept the stairs and the front door with the front garden clean (including the flowers), she would deduct even two hundred and fifty euros from my rent. The rent of the house was one thousand euros! In other words, I would have had to pay only one hundred and fifty euros, plus gas and electricity.

That was great!

Of course, I had accepted without hesitation. Besides, it was a big house that I was very curious about. She explained it so well that we were the only ones who lived in this house. We would have no other people as neighbors. I couldn't wait to see it. When she called, I hadn't bought my plane ticket yet because I didn't know when I would be back.

"I'll call you as soon as I get back for an appointment," I said.

But now I want to continue telling you about Aunt Meral and Uncle Osman. There will be some points on which I had to take notes, because I absolutely could not forget anything. While I was away, I had to focus all my thoughts on that.

At 01:35 everyone retired to their rooms, I was tired. But everything was going slower than I had thought, but it was going. So it was very good that I had booked my Türkiye trip for two weeks. Aunt Meral, who walked around me like a mother, I liked very much. It was a feeling I didn't know, the feeling of a mother's embrace. It was only years later that I could enjoy it again.

Thanks to my uncle Osman and the driver, I was able to do some important tasks. We had talked to the driver on the phone from time to time. He was also very helpful to me in the past after they sent me to Germany. These three important people were very valuable to me. As I had mentioned before, they were among my loved ones and those whom I protect. These three precious people are among those I could count with one hand.

Through the driver, I was able to contact the company that installed the security cameras. More precisely, there was a good dialogue and communication between the employee and the driver. So they gave me all the information, especially usage passwords, so I could watch all the cameras from my house. From now on, I could watch the camera footage at my home in Germany.

This would help me with my processes in my later projects. If you remembered, we had a famous lady Nalan. She could be called a cheat and a criminal or a snakehead. Many times I had fallen victim to her games. When the time came, everyone would get the receipt. My anger and resentment at some of the injustices she had done to me still did not subside. With some of them, although I had suffered harm and injustice, I could tell that my anger had subsided and calmed down.

Some of them, according to the laws and style of our constitution, should receive their just punishment. By going to the judiciary to confront them with their deeds. I wanted them to be punished. So I had to gather some evidence and some witnesses.

Now I had set the ball rolling, no matter how or where it fell. I let it roll ...

So I filed my criminal complaint again with the prosecutor's office on behalf of the family that kidnapped me (but this time in person). Then I thought, *what if they denied it again?*

Back in the garden next door, there was a girl who visited me when I was working in chains. I was thirteen, the girl was fifteen. We had taken a photo together as a souvenir. On my feet were the chains. When this image suddenly came into my mind, I rolled up my sleeves and set out with the chauffeur to find the girl next door.

There was one more problem that I had not thought of before. This occurred to me after we had already set off. *What if she recognized me?*

What if the family that had kidnapped me saw me? But we had maybe five hundred meters to go, it was too late. Anyway, *next time I had to change my image completely,* I thought.

Finally, I wore the sunglasses of the chauffeur for camouflage, in order not to be recognized. I quickly got out of the car and rushed to the door of our old neighbors so as not to be seen. I was so scared and angry at myself. When my head was so full, I forgot one of the most important things. Anyway, it had happened. There was no cure for the dead. I had to be more careful next time so as not to leave any marks.

The neighbor girl's brother opened the door, whom I asked about his sister. But he did not recognize me, although I had taken off my sunglasses.

"Who are you, please? Why did you ask for my sister?"

With a slight smile I replied, "We used to be friends, I lived here and moved away. I'm just passing through, I didn't want to go on without saying hello," I said.

At some point he called his sister to the door. But he had meticulously patterned me from head to toe, thinking I hadn't noticed. The girl next door asked, "Brother, who is it?" Slowly she approached, not recognizing me either.

After I moved to Germany, I had made some changes to my image. Besides, I was still a child then, I had changed. Now, years later, two mature ladies faced each other. Hesitantly, I introduced myself after that she had recognized me immediately.

"Oh, my dear! Where have you been? I have been thinking about you a lot. Come on, come in, come in quickly so they won't see you," she spoke frantically and warmly, then embraced me wholeheartedly. With this sincerity, I found myself in her house. We went into a room. With goodies, food and drink, she quickly set the table, she was very hospitable.

"I don't have that much time. The driver is waiting for me, I'm very busy, my time is short. I didn't want to disturb you but I also didn't want to leave without saying hello. Do you remember? We took some pictures back then. Can you give me one as proof?", I fell right into the door.

"What do you mean, of course? As always, I keep them in my albums."

Hastily she fetched the album. She had more pictures, more than I had thought. In two pictures I was posing with the girl next door. My feet were attached to this huge chain, and in the other pictures you could see me working in the back of the garden. That was very good. The girl next door used to be very nice and, as far as I could tell, still was.

Briefly, I said that I had filed a criminal complaint with the prosecutor's office, that I had asked them for some pictures for these reasons.

"Of course, take them all. I'll be your witness too," she offered immediately. She had a benevolent approach.

Without thinking twice, I accepted her offers. We had hastily exchanged our contact information. I knew there would be no secrets between us. "I need someone to come in and out of this house, "I told her frankly. "Here I am," she replied, without hesitation. I had loved playing with my cards on the table. That way everyone knew what position they were in.

Yes, I wore my heart on my sleeve. Before that I was nothing in this house, when I was thirteen everyone used me as a punching bag to punch. It was very bad, what a disgusting thing. It didn't occur to me. Most of all, I still didn't understand how they could do such a thing. The longer I stayed there, the more I thought about the past. As soon as my sentimentality passed, my anger toward that family rose. At the door, we said goodbye. I quickly put on my sunglasses and ran to the car. We drove off as soon as I got in.

It was better to change my image. At that moment, this thought came back to my mind. So I asked the driver for the hairdresser of my late mother Filiz.

"Well, let me drive you to the hairdresser," he said, then told me on the way. "At that time we got a bank card for you from the master of the house Mr. Hikmet. This bank card was bequeathed to you by your late father. Since that day, I have not touched this bank account until today. Because I know the situation of you and your siblings. I knew that one day you would return. Justice must be found. What is in the account is yours, and I don't even know how much it is. If you want, let's go there together after the barber shop, then you can find out for yourself."

It was a good news, I was surprised about that. There was a property that was bequeathed to us by our late father Hikmet and our late mother Filiz. They had houses, summer houses, vacation houses, villa, luxury yachts, some latest model cars and much more. They also owned the holding company with several hundreds of employees. Our older brother had taken this responsibility to run it after we were sent to Germany.

Since then, my brother had called my maternal aunt four times and my paternal aunt twice. So even after all these years, there were only six phone calls. I was angry about that, but I did not harbor anger against him as I did with some others.

So the driver had helped me again by phone. A friend of his who worked in the holding company's accounting department was able to track all income and expenses. He could access the holding company's accounts through the computer. He paid the workers' wages himself online. He was also responsible for the investments of some other holdings. That would open all kinds of doors for me.

Immediately I had to find a very good lawyer. A very, very, very good one, in fact. So I asked my uncle Osman for a lawyer, who replied, "I'll take you to our bloody Nigar."

"Bloody Nigar?", I asked.

"That's the lawyer's nickname," he explained with a smile.

So my new lawyer's nickname was bloody Nigar. She was right up my alley for my bloody affairs. Just because of her nickname, I had warmed up to her from the start. I also needed someone who was like that. So I called my Uncle Osman and asked for the closest date he could organize. For my sake, I could have talked to her right away.

After two hours of driving, I arrived at the hairdresser. Immediately I was greeted and served a drink, then I waited my turn.

Unfortunately, my image would not change with just a haircut. I had to make a complete renewal and take on a completely different personality. So I decided to go shopping after the visit to the hairdresser.

One dealt with my head, one with my feet and hands, yet another with my eyebrows. Of course, it was not exactly a relaxing feeling. Finally, five people tugged at me, all taking care of me at the same time.

In the end, I even wore false eyelashes. My finger and toe nails were filed and monochrome nail polish was applied. My hair was lengthened, so I wore from short to long again, in addition I had it dyed black. After the make-up was still hairspray applied, then I was ready.

Since I wanted to be surprised, I had towels hanging in front of the mirror, which they should now take away. I was very surprised at my reflection in the mirror. Immediately, I warmed up to my new image. My makeup style was very different this time. It brought out my blue eyes. I liked myself when I looked in the mirror for the first time. For the first time, I liked myself better that day with these changes.

With everything I prepared myself for the new life I would begin. With everything! Now and then the chauffeur was called for my brother's work. He was not available at certain times. He had also talked to my brother beforehand about driving Aunt Meral and Uncle Osman wherever they wanted and whenever they wanted. In this way, he could take me anywhere. It had definitely made my job easier. It was very comforting to know the chauffeur among the people who were close to me and sincere. He was one of my loved ones. With him I was in good hands.

After the hairdresser, we stopped at the bank that the driver had told me about. He gave me the EC card and asked me to look it up. There was a large amount of money in this account that was bequeathed to me by my late father. I was amazed at this, *how could family lawyers and our famous Nalan have overlooked this large amount of money?*

I confessed to him, "For a while I would use some of the amount from the account, it would help me a lot, but I will give you back what I bought with it as soon as possible, be sure."

It was not a loan for me, I could keep it. But I didn't. After the bank visit, we rushed to the boutiques. Since I was changing my image, I had to change everything, my whole style. I had already made this decision in Germany, only I made the implementation in Türkiye. So I had bought new clothes in many different models. Including accessories and shoes. It was a big expense but it was part of the necessary investments. After all, I had brought enough money. Since I did not know yet how high the expenses for my revenge contained, I reached for the bank account.

The next morning, I had to visit the public prosecutor's office again with the driver. Immediately, I had handed in the pictures as evidence. While I was at the hairdresser, the driver had the pictures reproduced by the photographer, because I wanted to have them with me, not only as evidence, but also for me. He then ordered a laptop that was set up to scale for me. All the programs and functions I needed that would make my work easier were saved. In a few days it would be delivered, then I would play my trump card with this Nalân and her family lawyers.

When we came home, Aunt Meral could not believe her eyes. For I stood before her as a completely different person. She knew it, but she had not expected me to make such a strong change. Although she knew that things would change from now on, she was also worried about me.

"Don't, don't, my child. Refer to God. Certainly, my Lord will punish them."

It was for the best, she was right, but they had not played harmless tricks on me like bell ringers. No, it was not joking indignation, but what they had done to me was terrible. Of course, my Lord will undoubtedly bestow justice that each of us deserves. I had never doubted it and never will. Criminals had to suffer their punishment even in this world. But my Uncle Osman thought like me, the driver too. Nevertheless,

Aunt Meral was worried that something might happen to me. She was like a mother to me in her heart.

Meanwhile, Uncle Osman had made an appointment with my new lawyer named bloody Nigar for tomorrow. On my schedule, I already had an appointment with the prosecutor's office in the morning, so I made one for the afternoon with the lawyer.

Due to my purchases, full bags had accumulated in the house. My task today was to restore order in the house. Aunt Meral had not forgotten the dishes I had loved from my childhood and had set the table with my favorite dishes. However, I found every meal of Aunt Meral's delicious, I did not distinguish any of her meals from the others. She was a special person to me from head to toe.

The chauffeur said, "I'll be late tonight." He had informed me that he had to drive my brother to a restaurant out of town after work. The driver was already pretty tired from the day, but he had to drive four different businessmen to dinner. However, he had recommended his friend for us to call if we needed a driver.

Having them all behind me had given me a lot of strength, yet they were not even aware of their good deeds. As many closed doors as there were, they were opened one by one. Thus, my work was made easier.

After dinner, my uncle Osman offered, "Today the tea is on me, I want to make my special herbal tea for our daughter today." So he quietly retreated to the kitchen. My Uncle Osman was an exemplary father. He certainly did not have the habit of leaving his family alone or going out alone. My Uncle Osman was a home and family man who took care of his job, his home and his family. Compassionate and fatherly was his virtue! Even though they didn't have children, they had real mother and father feelings.

While Uncle Osman was preparing our tea from the herbs he had grown in the villa's garden, Aunt Meral prompted me, "Come on, I'm excited to see what you've bought. Let's see what all you bought."

"With pleasure," I replied. Full of joy, I got up from my seat and pulled the new clothes out of the bag one by one to present them to her. My style was quite different this time. It was a business style.

Already in Germany I bought different clothes for one or two days.

My brother and sister welcomed my trip to Türkiye in the off-season. I wanted to send them to Türkiye for a season too, to my Aunt Meral. We had all decided that together. But I had to finish some of my work before I started my new job.

Time passed very quickly today. The evening was approaching. A heavy tiredness overtook each of us. We drank our tea, I even drank three glasses of the herbal tea that my uncle Osman had freshly prepared. Since I also like gardening, I had learned from my uncle Osman which plants he used and how he brewed the tea.

This tea had another special feature. It was very good to know its special side. Every evening after dinner, my late mother Filiz and my late father Hikmet drank a glass of fresh herbal tea from my uncle Osman at home.

When I came to my homeland, I also wanted to settle the inheritance issues of our biological, deceased father. I would not leave a brick to my stepmother, because she had not even earned that, let alone the house. I would also get over my stepmother. Everything would be settled in time.

While we drank our evening tea, we talked about all sorts of topics. What had we done and what still needed to be done?

Uncle Osman said, "You're going to the prosecutor's office tomorrow morning anyway. Settle the inheritance problem while you're in your native country."

I also brought up the custody of my siblings, which I had also taken over. To make things easier for me, I had the court decision translated from German into Turkish by a translator in Germany. It was a good idea, although it was close, these things had to be handled as well.

It was morning, I was putting on my very stylish business suit that I had just bought. My hair and makeup were done. Thinking it might be chilly in the morning, I put on my suit jacket, plus I had my shoulder bag and sunglasses in hand. Now I was ready to go. In an unexpected moment, Uncle Osman and Aunt Meral stood silently in front of me.

"Here my child, a little souvenir from us," they said, then opened a small ornate box in their hands and handed me a stunning visual gold necklace with sparkling stones. I had not expected such a surprise. My aunt Meral put the necklace on me and kissed my cheeks, while my uncle Osman gave me a kiss on my forehead. "May God protect you and bring your affairs to success. I hope so, my daughter," he said. The three of us had shared a very emotional moment in the hallway of the house.

The driver had been waiting for me. After saying goodbye, I left and we drove off. The driver had dropped my brother off at the Holding. Earlier, Aunt Meral and Uncle Osman had told my brother that they needed a driver. My brother's preference was always for his private workers. The coming and going of other or substitute workers bothered him. But I could also do my other business with the driver's friend who was suggested to me.

The weather was not as cool as I thought it would be.

"Your laptop will be ready in two days," the chauffeur informed me. Things were moving along steadily. We would be driving a long way again. It was about two and a half hours by car to the prosecutor's office.

There was to be my first date with my new lawyer named bloody Nigar in the afternoon. Everything went according to plan without any setbacks.

That's how I had presented my evidence to the prosecutor's office. "I had already filed a criminal complaint against this family. At that time, I was told that they were tribal families, and besides, the prosecutor was their relative. So therefore my denunciation was invalid and they turned it into compensation because I would have lied and misrepresented," I added to the subject.

It was very good of me to present the evidence, because the intervention began immediately. I wanted to see and experience this moment. There was no longer a small, helpless and powerless Yasemin. From now on, a mature and strong woman stood in front of them.

I wanted each of them to be punished according to Turkish law and justice.

I had also declared what my stepmother had done as a crime to the prosecution orally and in writing. My stepmother was also guilty.

These processes were not as short as I thought, but lasted quite a long time. We were now in a waiting area with the driver. Any moment now they would all be brought in front of the judge.

It was time to face it. I never thought it would happen so quickly.

Finally, I was ready to face these problems. Although years had passed, I tried to roll up the old pages, clean the stained pages and leave them clean.

Now I was brought in front of a judge and the excitement began. I had resubmitted my oral complaint, but also my written complaint. Beforehand, I had prepared it calmly in

Germany, because I knew that exhausting days would await me in Türkiye.

I could not believe my eyes. Years later, I was face to face with my stepmother. She was brought into the long corridor of the prosecutor's office, accompanied by two policewomen and a gendarme. Now I was no longer a small, offended, helpless, voiceless Yasemin. She was literally staring at me with her eyes. I didn't care if she stared at me, I really wanted her to receive the harshest punishment, just as she deserved.

My stepmother was convicted of four different crimes. Prison awaited her with open arms. But I didn't expect it to move so quickly. It didn't take long for the other criminals, the police and the gendarmes, to take them one by one to the prosecutor's office. So they were brought in front of a judge.

The neighbor who had given me the pictures also came to stand by me and support me. I never thought that she would be such a great help. Moreover, the neighbor had come in a hurry to testify without hesitation. Not only bad people entered my life, but also compassionate people with good intentions and humane approaches.

On my feet there were still the traces of the chains from my childhood, to which I was bound like an animal. They were scarred scars. Even a huge bull couldn't take a step of their weight, they were so heavy. These people had to pay for what they had done. I would devote all my strength and energy to punishing the people who had tortured and bullied me. They took the whole family to the prosecutor's office. Each of them was questioned separately. Criminals were punished, at any cost. They would take their punishment.

Anyway, I told the prosecutor's office that they could meet me at my German residence by letter. After almost five hours at the prosecutor's office, they let me go. The criminals were arrested and served their sentences one by one. At least for some of them, we considered this form of punishment sufficient and drove off again with the driver calmed down.

I was most pleased that Leyla was free as of now. This I would explain later more clearly and in more detail.

After we left the prosecutor's office, we also took care of our inheritance and headed for our house. I felt very comfortable, full of peace. While we still had an hour drive ahead of us, I called my aunt Meral. She was preparing lunch and waiting for us. After lunch, we had to leave immediately for my lawyer appointment. Time passed so quickly that we were running behind time.

After we ate our meals ...

The driver, Uncle Osman and I went to see my lawyer, nicknamed bloody Nigar. We waited in the waiting room to make the appointment at her office. Her office was located on a busy street right in the center.

It was our turn. Because of her nickname, I was very curious and excited about her.

When my name was called by the secretary, we went into her office and shook hands in greeting.

I honestly did not expect such a charisma. I told myself that she was both beautiful and successful. As for her nickname, we both burst out laughing as if to say "Great." A lawyer was a matter of trust. At first glance, we had felt sympathy for each other. This was a very important point for me.

Together we would achieve many successes. That was how I had explained everything to her from beginning to end. It had taken me quite a while to get to the last incident in the prosecutor's office. From now on, my lawyer would take care of all my affairs, up to and including my medical reports. From now on, we would work together head to head and shoulder to shoulder against the oppressors.

In the meantime, the husband of my paternal aunt, who lives in Türkiye, has been released. I had learned about this on my trip to Türkiye. He had been sentenced to one year and four months in prison, with a commuted sentence for alcohol consumption, instead of a serious prison sentence for rape. This did not seem sufficient to me. It was very insufficient.

In that case, everyone should drink alcohol beforehand and commit the crime they wanted. Oh, there's no way, I said to myself. The more I thought about how I went down after the rape and couldn't get up, the more vivid it became before my eyes.

What was a year for such people? I couldn't believe it, I kept repeating how a year and four months came about. This news made me nervous.

Now I wanted to retreat a little into my inner world. My notes had to suffice for the beginning, and I had reached the end of my volume anyway.

Woman; She is patient!
But when she breaks, she rips the tree out of
its roots with her storm.

Yasemin's Struggle

CHAPTER
6

It Was Tuesday!

Four days later, I wanted to return to Germany. Almost all my work was done, there was little left to do. It had been exhausting, of course, but I had also come to Türkiye to clean up my past, not to take a vacation. The changes I had made to my appearance had boosted my self-confidence.

In the meantime, I had received my laptop. All the necessary programs were installed on it, now I could work in peace. The person who had installed the programs had trained me in everything. I knew everything, right down to their passwords.

Even though I knew this was a crime, I used them anyway because now I had free access to the surveillance cameras at home and at work. This would make things much easier for me. I had resorted to this means to protect my brother from some people.

Through a private detective, our famous Mrs. Nalân was also exposed. At first I could not believe what I heard. Thinking *I needed proof for the accusation*, I had photos taken of her.

Mrs. Nalân was indeed a married woman, but I could not talk much about marriage because these issues were not on the agenda at that time. Her husband was a sports therapist in a rehabilitation clinic. When he received the wrong treatment, he became paralyzed and was completely bedridden for a while. During this time, when our adopted family, my mother Filiz and father Hikmet, had passed away, she officially separated from her husband that everyone knew about it, but in reality she had not separated. She had made such a despicable decision to implement her plan and project. She was a cheater.

I had been looking forward to this day, when I could convict her and she would pay a very harsh penalty. She was able to carry out her spiteful games, it had been a difficult time for all of us. Our family lawyer had divorced her at that time. As if her dishonesty had not been enough, I had even witnessed her clandestine relations with the family lawyer at the time. Their intention was to somehow seize my brother's assets. That was why they had committed such fraud. She wanted to wrap my brother around her finger and marry him just for his wealth. Of course, the fact that she had caught my brother at a very weak moment made it easier for her.

With that, this dishonest woman had achieved what she wanted: she had managed to get my brother to walk her down the aisle.

But she still hadn't left her husband, who was in need of care. They had a house and everything that went with it. Only officially they were separated, *but how could this dishonest woman use all these tricks?* Not only did she continue her secret relationship with the lawyer, but she had officially married my brother, while still being with her divorced husband. Through my brother, she had also started her own business and had moved up. She was on this and that television program. She was invited as a guest by all the stations and managed to stay on the screen from that day to this.

I had to find out where she lived with her first husband before returning to Germany. The rest was easy, because I had already put a detective on her, who would shadow her from now on. Sooner or later all the dirt would come out.

The fact that the detective was one of us made my material and moral work easier. With the help of my uncle Osman and the driver, the detective had accepted the assignment.

He did not even want to talk about a financial reward. With his short and concise sentence: "It's a question of honor," he concluded the topic.

This I could not accept, I insisted, "No way."

"I'm almost family. Whenever I'm needed, I'm with you as best I can," the detective replied with a sincere smile.

We had formed a nice staff. Our new team was to achieve extraordinary success. The people who accompanied me were people I trusted and believed in. This feeling was true for all of us.

There were so many good people who did not leave my side because they witnessed the injustices I had experienced. I did not let any of them come close to me anymore so as not to put them in danger.

Since I wanted to learn a lot about my brother, I asked Aunt Meral a lot of questions during our conversation. So I learned that he usually drank only on special occasions, not only on special occasions, that was not quite right. After my mother Filiz and father Hikmet died, he started drinking every day. Daily ...

He didn't stop until he was drunk. In the evening it was as if he was trying to put out the fire inside him.

For me, any kind of alcohol consumption was bad, in one form or another. This poison called alcohol can turn a person, even the most civilized person, into a wild animal. Therefore, I was not one of those people who said, "Drink to see what you are," like some other people. Also, I would like to give a message to every drinker from the bottom of my heart: "If you drink, don't drink too much".

As a thirteen-year-old child, I was forced to drink under duress. As a child subjected to violence and persecution, I was made to live a nightmare of being raped by a grown man. Alcohol is one of the most harmful and vicious gifts that can be recommended or offered. I would humbly advise you to keep those who approach you in this manner away from you.

Let's get back to our main topic!

Things had changed a lot. My return to Türkiye after many years was to be a lesson for some people. We had achieved more than I had expected: law enforcement was quite successful. It was shorter than I had expected, but of course it was very exhausting to tell everything from beginning to end, since I had submitted my statement in writing, they believed me. To my relief, the criminals were really arrested and would be punished by the justice system.

The person who had set up my laptop specifically for me was a genius. He had thought through everything, down to every program, and designed it from the ground up so that I could use it easily.

Now I had everything in my hand.

Even all the income and expenses of the holding company I could easily track. With the security cameras in the house and in the holding company, I could monitor everything from my laptop. I had to be prepared for the day when I would face my brother.

There were only a few days left until my return to Germany. Before my return, I wanted to meet the former neighbor's daughter once again. When she contacted me by phone, we arranged to meet.

She was brave, I did not want to lose her. Our meeting was sincere and trusting. We had a long conversation over dinner and talked about our problems. Without fear, even though she had not seen me again for many years, she testified to the prosecution without batting an eye, even though she was a neighbor of the criminals. *Isn't that true humanity?*

Today I had slowly started to pack my bags, because from now on my days would be quiet and relaxed. There was only one appointment left, and that was with my lawyer. She needed further proof that my siblings and I were adopted. That was absolutely no problem. I had not brought the documents to our first appointment, it must have slipped my mind.

At the prosecutor's office, I also learned that I did not have to appear at every court date. When my lawyer was called in, I was relieved that she herself appeared at the court dates and that I did not have to appear at every court date. Because I kept telling her that I did not want to be confronted with such despicable people and I was already living in Germany.

After our first appointment, my lawyer initiated all the necessary procedures. From now on, I could continue on my way without stopping.

Before I returned to Germany, I had to do some shopping in Türkiye. I had gone shopping in the center with my aunt Meral and uncle Osman. We had been on the road all day. After eating our fish at the restaurant, we had gone home tired. The house had been turned upside down by all the shopping bags.

Suddenly the doorbell rang. Aunt Meral hurriedly opened the door, and there stood my brother Nihat. But he definitely should not see me. Immediately I had hidden behind the door, because there was no other exit from the living room. The access to the other rooms from the hallway was free.

However, that was of no use to me at that moment. Therefore, I immediately signaled Uncle Osman. "Send him to other rooms somehow, so that I can get out of the living room," I said quietly.

Somehow, Uncle Osman managed to direct my brother Nihat into the kitchen and close the door. In the meantime, I took the opportunity to rush into another room, because after all I had been through, I could not use such an adrenaline rush.

Then they left the kitchen and went into the living room. I was relieved! But I was drenched in sweat from excitement. After a short visit, my brother left again.

He came to see if they needed anything and to ask how they were. My aunt Meral and uncle Osman loved my brother like their own child.

In the meantime, I talked to my siblings on the phone every day or we used a camera in Messenger. They surprised me every time with their maturity.

As soon as I would return to Germany, I would continue my work without interruption, I had another week off. But this was no vacation, because I had things to do that were sometimes more exhausting than working.

In Germany, more innovations were waiting for my siblings and me, and I was excited about that. It was as if the time had come to put everything in order. As soon as I arrived, my siblings and I wanted to visit the house my new employer had told me about. It would be easier for me to take care of these things if I didn't have to work, because then I wouldn't have time to take care of my business, that was the truth!

To be a woman; to be cut into pieces!

Yasemin's Revenge

CHAPTER
7

Today Was Saturday.

Finally I was sitting on the plane, it felt like I was coming back to Germany as a different person. Yes, after so many experiences, why shouldn't they change me? Experience makes a person mature. Now I was able to accomplish many things. I had a freshness in me that I had not known before. It was as if I had been cleansed of many things, a feeling I could not easily express. Perhaps it was a feeling I had never experienced before so I found it difficult to describe. In any case, I returned quite invigorated.

Everything had changed, even my image. I experienced an inner change, and I had become stronger. My new style also made me a different person on the outside. From beginning to end, I experienced the change. My self-confidence had increased.

The fact that some of the criminals had been punished had relieved me. The feeling that had always been there hurt me, because I had felt like a broken, helpless, poor, powerless person. Now there were none of those feelings anymore.

Thank God, I was no longer helpless either. I was no longer Yasemin, who had submitted to oppression for years. We no longer had to make decisions about our lives against our will and live with those decisions.

I was hurt a lot when I was a sapling and just beginning to blossom. Many times I was oppressed, I was attacked by people who uprooted me from my homeland. Each time I was alone with my pain, yet I took the responsibility of my siblings, because for them I endured every blow.

Even though I was writhing in pain, I was a strong character today. Yes, I could say that I was a strong character. I was able to survive any coup because I protected my siblings, God willing.

Even though the scars left by the coups still caused pain from time to time, the more I felt those pains, the tougher and stronger I became. So I could describe the difference in my feelings. I could say that this was my mental state caused by the current change.

The airport was close to our house. It was good that it was only thirty minutes away. After landing, I wanted to take a cab home. In my luggage I had surprises for my siblings, they would be very happy about that. If my luggage weighed more than thirty kilos, I would have to pay customs for the excess weight. This mishap had happened to me two weeks ago on the outbound flight.

The plane was slowly preparing for landing. Although my brother and sister had seen my new style and image in our video call, I was sure they would be very surprised when they saw it live. I was excited to see the looks on their faces when they saw the various small and large gifts I had for them. They would be very happy about that. Right now I was in a very happy phase. This change even triggered a feeling of happiness in me, because I had a never-ending smile on my face. It was a very nice feeling that with God's permission, after the first step I would take out of the door of this plane, a new life and a new Yasemin would take its place on the agenda.

I was very happy about that. This was my new life. With God's permission, everything was going well. It was as if all the closed doors were opening effortlessly one by one.

By now I had reached the end of both my cassette and my recording. We were already strapped in, the plane was landing. Today I had had an appointment with my late mother Filiz's hairdresser to have my makeup done and blow-dried before I left. After that, I had made an appointment with a photographer to have professional pictures taken. Almost one hundred and fifty photos were taken. Thirty pictures he had edited and put on a floppy disk. To this day, I had no pictures of myself alone.

Of course, I had not forgotten that there were photos of my late father Hikmet and my late mother Filiz, my siblings and me, which we had taken by a photographer. Before I was sent from Türkiye to Germany at that time, I was able to take them. They were special and were clearly visible at my home.

I would record my next voice recording from home. The plane had almost landed, I was so excited! Maybe that's why I couldn't get down to business today.

Goodbye for now ...

"Yes, Yasemin had reached the end of her recording and cassette at that point. That was very good news. I was very happy about that. She smiled when she spoke, I felt peaceful and happy listening to her. I was very happy for Yasemin, because these changes she was going through would make her a completely different person. That's why Yasemin was my hero. From the first day, she was always my hero.

Her unannounced departure had hurt me very much in those first days. It had hurt me as if a piece of my heart had been torn away. But the more I listened to the cassettes Yasemin had sent me, the more I appreciated them and left them to themselves: "Free soul," I said to Yasemin from time to time.

Let's continue with the sixth cassette that Yasemin had sent without further interrupting these changes, new developments and feelings in her life."

Even the worst mistake is not

as bad as never trying.

CHAPTER
8

A New Tuesday Had Dawned.

The ninth of December.

It was 00:13.

It was winter!

In the meantime, I had arrived home. My vacation was over and I resumed my monotonous life. Concentrating, I listened to the end of the sixth volume, because I wanted to pick up where I left off so there would be no confusion.

Yes, I said "Hello!" to this shiny new life with the first step I took when I got off the plane. Around 10:30 p.m. I was at home.

First I kissed and hugged my siblings tightly. Although I was very tired, I gave them the small and big gifts I had bought without making them wait any longer. They were both very happy.

Right in the evening I took all the things out of my suitcases and put them in their place. The things that needed to be washed, I immediately threw into the washing machine and washed them without waiting any longer.

Of course, in the meantime, our conversation with my siblings was not over; we were still talking about what had happened and what would happen in the future. For some reason, I was not hungry. Kiraz and Suat had prepared the food and set the table. They had waited to eat until I arrived.

Without waiting any longer, I seated them at the table and began to serve myself. We all smiled from time to time, it was a smile that would not rest.

Before I left for Türkiye, I had enrolled in a driving school. After my vacation, I wanted to start immediately. First they sent me to a first aid course. It lasted almost eight hours. After I received the certificate of participation in the first aid course, I attended the written lessons. After I had completed twelve hours, I was told that I could take the written exam. It looked like it was going to take longer than I thought, but somehow I had to get through it before we moved away.

During my vacation, I had made an appointment by phone with my new employer about her mother's house. We were able to schedule it for a weekend because I definitely did not want my siblings to miss school. My siblings and I were very curious about the house. It was going to be a change for all three of us.

So I had rented a room in the same hotel again, and at my request that my siblings and I stay in the same room, they had additionally put folding beds in the room. To avoid any stress, we left a day before the appointment, so we met my new employer in front of her workplace in peace the next morning.

We were in a good mood. My new employer had noticed my new style right away. One of the first things she mentioned was the change. After she met my siblings and shook their hands, we all walked to the house together. We had been walking for almost fifteen minutes. The house was in the city, but it was still somewhat secluded even though it was in the center. That was even better.

Her mother was not there yet, who owned a hair salon on the first floor of the house. My siblings and I were to live upstairs if we liked it. If not, we would still make it our own. There was no way I was going to pass up an offer like that. I was one hundred percent sure of myself; I was determined, ambitious, and hardworking as long as my health permitted. My siblings were no longer small, so I had no doubt that they would settle in.

My new employer said she had the keys to the house, but she wanted her mother to show us everything, so we waited for her. She had told her mother a lot about me. She especially emphasized that I was determined and ambitious, that I lived alone with my siblings and that I wanted to change cities.

I thought to myself at that moment that she didn't need to know other things anyway.

Since the waiting time was very long, my new employer opened the door of the hair salon.

"Come on, at least you can already see the hair salon and the backyard with garden," she suggested.

The backyard was never mentioned. "It is impractical, my mother can no longer take care of it because of her age," she explained.

It was a hair salon that had been in the hands of her mother for fifty-seven years. Although the salon was old, it was busy. Of course, it was not as big as my new workplace, but the furniture had a very special design choice. I liked it ... After all, this hair salon was going to be my workplace, if only for one day a week.

My new employer was very warm and friendly to me and my siblings. She made me feel that she trusted me. She trusted us, although she did not express it, it showed in every mood and situation.

She opened the back door of the hair salon. My siblings and I couldn't believe what we saw, it was a huge backyard with a beautiful garden. But, as they hadn't used it, they hadn't mentioned it. I could turn this garden into a perfect paradise. With great joy and curiosity we went inside.

Although Kiraz, Suat and I had not yet seen the inside of the house, we liked it very much so far. I was facing the garden and was busy inspecting it, with the house behind me. As I turned around, I thought to myself that this must be a balcony terrace. The apartment we would be moving into had two floors. On the second floor of the house there was a huge roof terrace overlooking the garden, you could actually call it a balcony. This house was really like winning the lottery. We were very happy.

When her mother arrived, we greeted each other and shook hands after introducing ourselves. Her mother, like her daughter, was one of the fancy ladies; although old, she was a very well-groomed lady. As a family they had been faithful to the family profession for years. She had inherited this hair salon from her mother's mother. So they were in the fourth generation. The son of my new employer also worked together with his mother in the salon.

Four generations was easy to say.

After we had finished our conversations in this way in the garden, we slowly went into the house. Her mother had explained and shown us everything, down to the smallest detail. We went up the stairs to our house.

Only we would live in this huge house. When we were still on the stairs, I came to talk about the garden: "Your garden has been a little neglected, if you allow me, I would like to take over all the work in the garden and make it usable. The garden has not been touched for a long time, I can create a very beautiful paradise garden here. I have a lot of experience in gardening and would like to take you a step further. In the beginning we may have some expenses."

Euphoric, she replied, "Whatever you need, you can tell me. I'd be happy to!"

Oh, how nice, we would have a garden from now on. This garden was even bigger than the garden of my current house. It was almost eight hundred square meters, not counting the sitting areas.

As I climbed the stairs, she showed me a small room where all the cleaning and gardening equipment was stored. I was told that the stairs and walls had been rebuilt and painted just a few months ago. Yes, it was obvious that everything was spotless. She said the house had been vacant for a long time and she had renovated and refurbished everything. From the tiles of the house to the shower stall, the bathroom to the sink and the cables / sockets, everything was new. Of course, that was even better for us.

Arriving at the door of our new house, my excitement increased. My siblings and I held hands tightly. The door was opened and we all entered the house. All the floors in the house were brown. There was a shiny parquet floor. Every room was beautiful and large. We had especially liked the kitchen, it was huge. The best part was that the kitchen was newly installed. It was a brand new white high gloss model kitchen. It looked like a palace to me. The almost thirty square meter balcony could be accessed from both the kitchen and the living room. It was a beautiful house, we had just toured the lower floor. At the entrance of the house there was a second corridor, from which you could get to the second floor.

On the second floor was the living room, kitchen, bathroom with shower stalls, two hallways and an empty small room. On the second floor there was a large toilet with two bathrooms and a shower room with two sinks next to each other. There were three medium sized rooms. This house was like a palace.

Everything had been renovated as if it had been prepared especially for us. From now on, Kiraz and Suat would have separate rooms, plus a living room that they would share. I wanted to leave the upper floor entirely to the two of them. The corridor on the second floor was continuously glazed, almost like a balcony door. This offered a very nice view.

My siblings' living room had the aforementioned roof terrace. The small room on the first floor would be mine.

"Why didn't you rent the house out earlier?", I asked in amazement.

The previous condition of the house was very poor. On the walls there were green and brown wallpapers from long ago. From the sockets to the floor of the house, everything was very old and absolutely unusable.

The house previously belonged to the grandmother of my new employer. When she died three years ago, her mother inherited it. When she tried to rent the house in its old condition, those who visited it several times did not like it, so it was not rented. When the house was empty in this condition for two and a half years, she found it necessary to renovate the house from scratch and after six months of repairs, we were the first to visit the house.

We talked again about the house and the work I should do. Everything that was financially and emotionally necessary was discussed, she also accepted my idea of organizing the garden.

"I guess at this rate I'll be paying you monthly, not you paying me," she joked.

My expenses were minimal, they were limited to water, heating, electricity and a very small amount of rent. It was great. There could not have been better news for me. My siblings were just as happy as I was.

They didn't just want a tenant, they wanted someone who would take care of the house and keep it clean. What could be easier than that. The house was just right for us.

After we had agreed on everything, we shook hands again: "Okay, then I will prepare the lease. Then I'll send it to your current address," she offered.

All the doors opened one after the other, without any difficulty. The house was perfect, even if it was remote, it was fifteen minutes from my new workplace. Close to the schools where my siblings were going to go. I was very happy, and our new house was more beautiful than we expected. It was like a palace, as if I were in a dream world. I had experienced so many setbacks during my life, and now, with God's permission, everything was going very well for my siblings and me.

Everything changed in our lives. The feeling of happiness that came in these last few days because of these changes could not be described. For the first time in my life, I tasted that feeling of happiness. For the first time. I felt that I now knew that I had arrived in life. I felt that I was alive.

May God preserve and protect us from even more severe trials.

After about twenty minutes of chatting in front of the house, we all headed out, because there was no need to rush, everything was going according to plan and we had everything ready for our return trip.

After an almost five-and-a-half-hour drive, we arrived home at around half past six in the evening with a very good feeling. My siblings also liked the house very much. Kiraz and Suat immediately said, "We will also work in the garden," laughing. The happiness that day was really priceless.

Happiness is free, but still priceless.

CHAPTER
9

Within a few days I received the rental agreement for our new house in the mail. Only too willingly I had signed it and sent it back. In addition, I had also given her the cancellation agreement for the house we were now living in. I had to deal with the moving company. Actually, these movers were a very good thing; they took everything out and put it back in, right down to the lamp. They put the furniture up, they did everything if the money was right.

For the new house I wanted to buy new furniture. I wanted my siblings' rooms to be new, but also the dining table for our kitchen. Even the TV I wanted to replace and do it all in one day. I didn't want to take the furniture we were now using in the old house, just the new ones we had bought over time. The rest had always been used furniture, but that was better than nothing.

The first floor had been empty for almost five months now. So I had talked to the old landlord, I wanted to put the new small and large items I wanted to buy in the empty apartment until we moved. Without any problems, he gave me the keys to the apartment. We could now gradually pack what we didn't need into moving boxes, cassette them down and store them on the second floor. It was supposed to be a clean move.

After school, my siblings and I went out to buy furniture and electrical appliances. From now on, everyone would have their own private room and living room. That meant we needed new furniture. We were going to start a new life from scratch. I had bought special shiny stone tiles for the kitchen. The shiny stone designs on white would be perfect. The lamps were also made of shiny stone.

Actually, my dream was a magenta white kitchen, but I had bought a lot of magenta decor. We had bought my siblings' bedrooms and guest rooms, from rugs to televisions, and put them on the second floor of the house.

For everything I had spent a lot of money. The contract with the moving company still had to be prepared; I had to write everything down on paper, such as what was to be installed and set up in the new apartment. Therefore, I wanted to buy everything in advance, so that the craftsmen would not have any problems with the installation and assembly of the furniture on the day we moved in.

These were the new changes in our lives. Everything was changing, as you have read. Nothing would be the same as before. In my own inner world, extraordinary changes began to take place.

It was refreshing to talk, as if all the knots were being untied little by little as I spoke. I was no longer the poor, helpless, abandoned Yasemin, but a new side and a new Yasemin, who had been hiding in new continents and opening her eyes to the world, was now looking back at me in the mirror. In those days, these two different people were fighting with each other.

One was dead, one had awakened!

To one I will say "goodbye" and to the other "hello, welcome"!

*If people knew how much their
thoughts affected their health,
they would either think less or think differently.*

Yasemin's Struggle

CHAPTER
10

In the next few days I would take the written exam of my hairdressing profession. But I couldn't study much, so I hoped that I would pass my written exam without any mishaps. My vacation was already over, I had accomplished more in that time than I could have imagined and I could get things on track. So I had gone to work not with my head full but with my head empty. I had discarded everything that lay on my stony path.

I had already warned my siblings that I would neglect them both a bit in the coming days, but that we would cope with this situation. The driver's license, the written exam for my job, other paraphernalia for the move, the rest of the paperwork, my job ... was a lot. Of course, I had to prepare for stressful days.

Since I wanted to continue my profession at my new job, but there were differences between the states, I would possibly receive different vocational training. *"No matter,"* I told myself at that moment, what changes I had seen and experienced, this change was nothing compared to the other changes.

In between, I learned that my current workplace had organized a farewell party for me. I was happy about that, but I obviously wasn't ready for a surprise party, because I had to take care of everything else myself after work. Time was short, days were short. On top of that, I had two more written exams that were related to my job. One of them I would have to pass here in the next few days, and my last exam would be at my new workplace.

For my driver's license preparation, I had to take three more theoretical hours because my hours were not yet full. After my written exam, I wanted to start driving immediately and not lose any more time.

Once again, I was nearing the end of my recording. In my next cassette, I would talk about our developments.

Whatever you really fight for,
it will surely come to a conclusion!

CHAPTER
11

Today was the 12.25.2008

Christmas Holiday of Christians!

In our religion this was not allowed, but I loved these Christmas markets and Christmas. How carefully they prepared everything and decorated their colorful lights with love. The whole way to their houses was decorated with colorful lights.

Finally, I had passed both exams, including the written one for my driver's license. Now I wanted to start driving right away. Time was short and seemed to be running out. I had not yet received any notification of the written exam in my profession. So I thought that the notification would already arrive at my workplace in the next few days.

It was snowing, one had a wonderful view. The new furniture we had bought was about to be delivered to the second floor of the house. If a new tenant came at any moment, I would be lost.

We were going to stay here until 01/23/2009, then move. Because I was planning to take advantage of the last two and a half weeks by using the vacation days that were left over from my annual leave last year, since I would have a lot of work.

All the work consisted of taking care of my siblings and me.

The people who could help us were also limited in our near and far surroundings. Since the new place we were moving to was pretty far away, that was impossible anyway. So the moving company had been a really good decision.

It was getting more hectic by the day, because I had to get my driver's license before we moved. Time passed so quickly that it was really surprising.

Yesterday I had done the housework with my siblings. Today we had a complete break in our daily schedule, so it was a quiet day. I wanted to spend the day with my siblings. We have been busy the last few days and could see a good movie on TV. At the same time, I was watching the surveillance camera footage on my laptop that I had brought from Türkiye.

About a week ago, the detective had sent me an e-mail. In it he told me that he had found the address of the house where Mrs. Nalân lived with her first husband. Until today, she had not left him. That day I also learned that her first husband had never visited the house where they lived together. He had also sent some pictures. There was a picture of Mrs. Nalân and the family lawyer sitting in the car talking, but that didn't have to mean anything.

Just now I was thinking about Nurgül, so I wondered if I could give her these recordings one day? Or had I recorded them all for nothing, talked to myself for nothing? Nevertheless, I continued my recordings without interrupting them, as if Nurgül existed. Who knew how many times she had tried to reach me? After changing my phone number, I had called her twice without speaking and without giving my number. She had said, "Hello, hello!" then hung up. In retrospect, I found that this behavior did not suit me at all.

Sooner or later, God willing, I would tell her everything calmly when the time came. I was sure that she would understand me.

Our neighbors were not home for the Christmas holidays. There was no one in the house except us. I wanted to dismantle the furniture that we didn't want to take with us one by one and put it on the second floor that was empty for the time being.

That day we had worked for six hours. Although I should have felt tired, I felt a sense of relief, as if we had finally finished the rough work. After that, I spent the rest of my time with my siblings, enjoying ourselves.

It was only one week until the move ...

To speed up my driving license, I took driving lessons twice a day from time to time. I learned everything quickly and had no difficulty in applying it. Of course, I made many mistakes during my first attempts. *Who didn't have that?* Tomorrow would be the last two driving lessons. After that, my mandatory hours were through. "Sign me up for the first available date for the test," I had discussed with them.

"No problem, it depends on how fast you study, we can do it on the same day," my teacher had replied and signed me up for the test on the last day of the week. He told me that I could pick up my driver's license at the municipality of the new city we would move to.

By the way, while we were talking about the exams, I had also received the news that I had passed the written exam of my hairdressing profession. After all the exams, I had exactly one year left until the end of my professional training. I wanted to get through the hard days quickly ...

If you want something from the heart,
it's a must.

CHAPTER
12

Three Weeks After I Moved In.

I had listened to my last recordings only briefly; it was as if I were keeping a diary. By letter I had received notification that I had passed my driver's license test. Now I could pick up my driver's license at the municipality.

Yes, you read that correctly. We had moved into our new house, our new home.

With the moving company we had moved without any problems. They had also set up our new furniture and put our lamps in place. All we had to do was unpack the packages, hang the curtains, put the rugs down and put everything in its place. Our house was as good as new.

On my first day of work, *I had told myself how glad I was to have shopped in Türkiye,* because it made it seem like my work colleagues were all dressed like celebrities and businesswomen. They were meticulously groomed. Of course, I had to keep up with my new business life and still expand my wardrobe in every way.

What worried me the most was the fact that my siblings had to change schools several times since they arrived in Germany. Although they did not complain about it, I was annoyed.

They got used to new environments very quickly. I think it was because they had never known anything different from their childhood until that age. They were both used to starting their lives all over again. Life had accustomed them to it.

Our house was close to everything, apartment, school and shopping center. In this respect we were very lucky, we were very happy with all the recent changes.

Despite everything, I had to focus on my goals. These preparations began with the fact that I first had to be strong. I had to become stronger first, and through these changes I became stronger day by day. I felt that way.

Mrs. Nalân could not continue her games. There were still a few people I had to show my trump card to. With Mrs. Nalân alone, the work was not yet done, but I first had to get used to and adapt in every way to my new workplace, our new house and the city to which we had just moved. We had divided the work in our house among the siblings, since it would be unfair to divide all the work among one person. But this issue had never caused any problems between us siblings.

My siblings were as precious as diamonds to me until today. *Thank God,* they had never given me any trouble. In this respect, I was very lucky because not everything can go wrong in life. I had a great advantage in terms of my job. Why?

To better train her employees, she sent them to seminars in all areas of hairdressing. This was very good for us. At the end of the seminars we received certificates of achievement or diplomas and the nice thing was that we could participate in competitions. The trophies of my new employer, who was twice a world champion, were the eye-catcher in the salon. Her diplomas, certificates and other awards hung on the walls of her salon. There were many other certificates and many other things, including Golden Scissors awards. I also learned that she had entered us in such competitions, which was great. I was very happy about this news.

This was the best opportunity for us to continue our education and development. I was very happy about that, I never regretted this step and probably never will.

My days were quiet because first we had to lay the groundwork for our new environment, our new home, our new business life and our new school world. I let everything happen and it happened as it was supposed to happen. I was quite successful at my job so I was sure that in time I would make it big.

Only those who are with you in your bad time have earned the good that is with you.

Yasemin's Struggle

CHAPTER
13

Today Was the Beginning of Spring!

Even though the weather was a little windy, the sun made for a good mood. Today was a very special day for me even if there was no reason, it was just a feeling. My mood and morale were very good. It had to be because of the energy of the sun. Of course, I wanted to use it. So I hope that others would also benefit from this positive energy because I thought that the more objective we think, the more positive energy would fill our body.

Today Germany resembled a Sunday; it was a (religious) holiday for the Germans. The weather was great. After an energetic breakfast, I wanted to get started on my first gardening project. Until now, I had never thought about *how I wanted to design the garden.* All sorts of ideas were flying around in my head when I first got my hands on the garden.

I could plant this here and that there. This would look good here. Actually, this felt like organizing a house. All the materials needed for the garden were stored in an empty room near the stairs that led from the hallway to my apartment.

My siblings were awake. Actually, they would probably sleep an hour longer because of the holiday, but they both woke up from my noise. Not wanting to offend either of them,

I greeted them with a smile and a kiss, "Good morning, my darlings."

On Sundays, our breakfast table was quite lavishly set. In other words, whatever God had given us. We attached great importance to Sunday breakfast, we took more time than on other days. I also attached great importance to the appearance, because after all, the eye ate with us.

On weekdays, we were all in a hurry to get ready because of work and school. Out of haste, we put something in our mouths and went on our way. Now, this was Germany, where work and school life began at the crack of dawn before it got light. It was a disciplined and bureaucratic country; I liked these characteristics of Germany very much. But it was not only a bureaucratic country with a proper system, it was also an exemplary country.

After breakfast, I started gardening with great joy and good humor. My siblings helped me to carry all the necessary materials. Of course, I was prepared, I had already bought the seeds of everything that was planted this season. First I had to turn the garden completely upside down. While working in the garden, I found a lot of peace, which did me good. It was like I could rest like that. That day I spent almost the whole day in the garden.

Why had I started to describe my days in such detail lately?

Lately, yes, after these recent innovations, I felt a joy, peace, and refreshment within me. I felt relief, both from the changes I had experienced about myself and from my plans of revenge that I would implement in the course of time. I wanted to share these feelings with you.

What an important feeling, what an indispensable feeling!

I felt relieved because I knew that those who had treated me cruelly would be punished in due course. It was as if justice was being served. When you found a place of equilibrium in your mind, that inner relief was reflected on your face with a smile. With a smile, you could show that you were happy.

But I was a sullen and unhappy person before the right was fulfilled. "So do not remain silent about the offences committed. Do not submit to the injustices done to you. Intervene, even if not everything is done immediately and in time, one day justice will prevail. The guilty will be punished. When that time comes, do not be silent! Defend your rights", this is the message I would like to convey to you as it was going through my mind just now. As someone who had experienced victimization myself, I want to convey this message to you. I felt like I was living and feeling human for the first time.

By now we had reached the end of the seventh volume. It seemed that Yasemin was making more and more rational decisions and becoming more mature. Yasemin's peers, however, were not living the life that Yasemin was living. They were people from other worlds. For Yasemin had always dealt with people older than her and she could always communicate with them. Her experiences had matured Yasemin, whether she wanted them to or not.

Eight years had passed since she had prepared these records for me. Exactly eight years later, she sent me these cassettes, numbered one by one. Wasn't that interesting?

As you can see from the content of the recordings Yasemin had made eight years ago, as she herself had mentioned several times, she had become more and more self-confident, grounded and quite strong due to the changes she had gone through. Now capable of standing on her own two feet, she was an intelligent young woman. If Yasemin had felt these feelings eight years ago and had changed in this direction, can you imagine how today, eight years later, she was one of the people who had a say?

Even though I never had contact with her, these feelings came up in me, "Eight years ago, eight years later." I just want to say, "It would be appropriate." I certainly wasn't wrong in thinking that. Time would tell everything, because I was sure it would be. We will wait and see together...

A week ago, Yasemin had sent me cassette eight, nine and ten. This time I could continue my work without interruption. Now that three cassettes arrived together, it could take longer for me to finish.

After the eight-year break in "Yasemin's Revenge," she had established a different system of working with me. We weren't in contact like we were then, but I had the feeling that her return would be phenomenal.

Cassette eight was a special message to me. When I started listening to it, I said, "Oh no, this is amazing!" I was very touched because she had made me very happy with this beautiful surprise.

In terms of content, she expressed some wounds that she did not want to mention in the book project. It was almost as if she was talking to me. It was as if she was pouring out her heart. Yasemin seemed to have really changed. These changes she had experienced were reflected in her speech and tone. Her tone and the different phrases she used had won me over immediately. Let's look together at how Yasemin had become a new "ME" day by day and had experienced further changes.

A word; it can change a person's life!
Read it and don't shut up!

Yasemin's Struggle

CHAPTER
14

In fact, I had a very active day today. Before I left for work in the morning, I had sent an e-mail to Nihat's e-mail address on condition of anonymity. In it, I had sent the research results and information about our famous Mrs. Nalân, in other words the wife of my stepbrother Nihat. I had also added the photographs taken by the detective as evidence in a file. I had uncovered their fraud one by one. In my message, I had clearly written that he had been deceived.

He would be very shaken by this mail. Maybe he would have followed up on this incident to investigate it himself. Maybe my mail would open his eyes. Hopefully, he would realize what was going on. Since she was under close surveillance, sooner or later I would find out her reaction to my email.

This woman Nalân was in fact a swindler, a forger, a cheat. This woman should pay a heavy fine. This time the detective was looking for evidence of crime, to find it he was going to call a close friend of his who worked in the financial department of the holding company and whom we had met through our driver. He had already organized my laptop. Thanks to him, I could see the security camera records online, and the inputs and outputs from the holding company's account were invisible to anyone. This person had been very useful to me.

I had asked him to check the remarkable expenses. The investigation revealed that things were deeper than we thought. The more I dug, the more things came to light. A shameful woman! As soon as I had evidence, I sent it to my brother's email address without batting an eye. From then on, whenever I found an evidence against Nalan, I sent it to him.

A few days later, I had a phone conversation with my aunt Meral. Because I wanted the emails (pictures, proofs, documents, papers ...) that I had sent to my brother to be put in an envelope on the desk in his office. Therefore, I wanted to send them to the address of the house in the center of Aunt Meral. I was very angry with my brother, but I wanted him to realize it himself. After all, at that time he thought I was out to get him. Of course, I just wanted to help but when I had told him, he hadn't cared. Okay, times were different. I admit it!

When my father Hikmet and my mother Filiz had died, my brother's inner world had also been in turmoil. Like all of us. Mrs. Nalân had given my siblings and me to my aunt, who lived in Germany, in exchange for money and my brother had played the three monkeys. Not seeing, not hearing, not speaking, as if then it was not the truth what had happened. We had been sent to my aunt in Germany against our will.

After that, we lived for three years in the basement, in a damp, dirty, rusty and dark room.

We still had to play our trump cards with this woman called "Auntie", but all in good time.

Thank God we had survived those days. My experiences were strung together like pearls on a necklace. The cruel things to which I had been exposed without rest had never left me in peace. But now the problem was solved, thank God. I had survived those days, with God's permission I had shaken it off in the hope of never experiencing anything like it again. Now I could erase the bad memories from the past from my life day by day.

Maybe I wouldn't manage to shake it all off, but at least I would be able to process most of it. So one day I could go on with my life as a new Yasemin. Maybe ... I had to live and wait ... Even if I didn't know yet what to expect. Time would show everything. Maybe I would take a completely different path, not at all the way I had imagined.

Stories of experience can sometimes be inspiring.
Read!

Yasemin's Struggle

CHAPTER
15

Three Months After Moving!

My new employer had signed me up for an award-winning European bridal hairstyle and updo competition. I was very excited about that because it was going to be my first competition. The contestants came from all over Europe and each year it was also held in a different European country. *"Oh my god"*, I thought to myself, I had to create an extraordinary design for that day. Of course, sometimes I had prepared for the competition during work or after my working hours.

Depending on which country had won the European Championship, the competition was held in that country the following year. This time it would be held in Belgium.

The day knocked on the door. Together with my employer and my model, we arrived in Belgium for the European competition. We stayed in a hotel. With every fiber of my body I was ready for the competition, which took place on stage with the model. It went really very well, I left the competition as the runner-up of the European Championship ... It was incredible ... Even though it was my first competition, they had deemed me worthy of second place.

This was a start and a success for me. Although I was still in training, I was very motivated by this result. My second place was hung in the salon next to the other prizes. It was a feeling of happiness and honor.

Just as I had begun to lay a foundation in Türkiye, I also had to lay a foundation in Germany, which I had now begun to do. The training period had exhausted me a lot. So I could not attach much importance to other things. I swam and swam, I had not yet reached the end of this intensive time. Now it was still a few months until the end. Again and again I told myself that I would get through these days just like the other days.

I would get through it ...

I had received a message from Aunt Meral that my letter had reached them. The letter was secretly placed on my brother's desk at the holding company. It contained some very important information that would enlighten him and bring him to his senses. My brother would recover and get back on his feet.

He had to face some truths but he also had to see some truths to come to his senses.

Maybe it was like a slap in the face, maybe when he saw it for the first time it would hurt him so much that he would withdraw completely into himself. He would reach a whole other dimension but he had to take off the glasses that had blinded him, he had to take them off to be able to face the truth. As in other matters, we will wait and see.

Let me describe my brother's office floor in the holding company so that you can better imagine what I am about to tell you. In the center of a city in Türkiye, on the 24th floor of a high-rise building (skyscraper), in an area of about one thousand eight hundred square meters, imagine a floor that was equipped with the most visual, largest, beautiful and eye-catching fashionable office furniture (white glossy). For the entrance; reception and consultation area, there were usually four staff members responsible for this area. Switchboard, reception, meeting services, etc. ...

A little further down the corridor, the passage divided into a right and a left branch. If you went a little further, the corridors merged into a round shape. In this part there were small and large offices, the number of which I did not know. The decor of this floor was magnificent. The inner wall of the two corridors, divided into a left and a right corridor, was made of thick glass through which water flowed in the form of a waterfall. The interior wall of the round part of the whole corridor was designed in this way by the interior designer. Behind a concrete wall was the canteen of the five different floors of the high-rise building, which belonged to the holding, as well as the toilets.

The other part of the skyscraper was designed in the same way. This part was my brother's office. Without having to enter the office, one reached the reception, as well as the chief secretary. To which one went through a short corridor.

The seat on which he sat was almost like a Sultan's chair. This explanation was figurative so you can get an idea.

Now imagine my brother in his own office. In the morning he would approach his desk, perhaps in a lively and half-awake state. After placing his bag somewhere, he would discover the letter. Surprised, he would open the letter, turn the envelope front and back again. Then he would look at the pictures one by one in a confused state.

Further, I imagined him saying, *"What is this?"* After reading it, he slumped down on his chair that resembled that of a Sultan. For a minute or two he could not move in his seat. In his seat, he read the short text again, squeezing it between his palm, then looked at the pictures again and suddenly stood up. After adjusting his tie, plus his jacket, he left his office and asked his secretary at the reception desk, "Who left this letter on my desk?"

The secretary replied, "I don't know!" Without stopping, my brother walked with quick steps to the first reception and consultation area, when he did not receive a clear answer there either, he returned to his office.

After telling the security guard on the phone that he would like to see the footage from the surveillance camera, he looked at the footage. However, since these images had already been deleted or were not recorded, he could not find any clues. After that, there were some private phone conversations about this issue ...

Yes!

As I expected, my brother had not seen the emails I had sent him and behaved as I had hoped he would when he received the letter. Even though it was bitter, it was the behavior I wanted and expected from my brother. The truth was bitter, unfortunately. Of course, I was very sorry for my brother but the time to realize the truth had already come and passed.

My brother was searching for the author of the note left behind. Every day he went new ways to find out the truth. Within a few days, he saw the truth with his own eyes and caught his wife Nalân in her other life with the creature who was considered the family lawyer. In the heat of the moment, just in time. "Nalân!" he shouted. Now *that's what I call a real confrontation,* I thought to myself.

He had seen the true face of this creature, who was one of the holding company's lawyers and was also known as the family's lawyer, with this note I had sent him. About that, I was very happy that from now on there would be no more people who would anger my brother. I did my best to make sure that my brother would see the truth. I was blessed with my Lord's approval to make even the impossible possible.

Based on these facts, he immediately filed for divorce with Mrs. Nalân. Undaunted, he returned to his business life. But one of the known problems was that Mrs. Nalân would have a lot to do with my brother in this separation matter. The outcome was not yet known.

In view of these developments, I was very relieved, I could not even describe it. Although my brother had ended his relationship with Mrs. Nalân, I was not finished with her. That was the first step I had planned. I was still waiting for the day when Mrs. Nalân would be dragged into the gutter. Mrs. Nalân was always present in the television programs. For example, my brother, who was one of the well- known and respected businessmen and Nalân, who was a guest on the TV programs, announced their divorce in the press. So it was not a secret affair. Everyone had witnessed this separation.

After this news, I returned to my daily life. Even if it was only for a few days, I had to focus on my personal and professional life again.

Most people say they care about the truth.
Until I hear it.

CHAPTER
16

Two Weeks Later!

Today was Sunday and I was very tired because I had cleaned the hairdressing salon, the stairs, the hallway and really worked in the garden for a total of seven hours without interruption. Now I relaxed in the garden with a cup of tea, fortunately the weather was very nice. My siblings had gone to the movies so I was alone. After a little rest and my shot, I would roll up my sleeves again.

Last night I had a long conversation with my aunt Meral via video call. Finally I had gained some new information again. My brother had a long talk with Uncle Osman in the garden after a shift. There had been emotional moments. Uncle Osman and Aunt Meral had such great rights over my brother as a mother and a father. Just as Aunt Meral was a mother to us in her time, she was to my brother with the same feeling and look. He had experienced more parental affection than we had. After some time, we were sent to Germany against our will. This feeling remained as a taste for us. My brother poured out his heart to Uncle Osman. After my brother had finished his last sentence, Uncle Osman had given him the following advice which my aunt reproduced to me one-to-one on the phone:

"Look, my son, you have become a great man. For years we have taken care of your late father Hikmet and your late mother Filiz. My wife was not your nanny but was and is as warm and close to you as a real mother. You grew up in her hands, you are a son to us. Okay, we are fulfilling our services here, separating one from the other.

As for your wife, I know where I belong and I want you to know that I don't want to go too far. We respect whatever decision you make. If you remember, Aunt Meral talked to you in the early days. Years have passed, you may have forgotten. But even if you don't think about her, your sister Yasemin also talked to you before she was sent to Germany. They both wanted to wake you up to protect you from your dishonest wife but without going too far. They had these conversations without going too far and in a way that respected your judgment.

It went in one ear and out the other. Is that a lie, my son? You don't call your step-siblings who live in Germany anymore. Are they doing well with their aunt, how are they? Don't you call and ask how they are? Do you call and ask, my son? I hesitate to go too far, my son, to be honest but this woman who has become your wife has done no good by sending them away. Has it never occurred to you where she found her aunt, why she gave her a large sum of money, why she sent all three of them away against their will to get rid of them in a hurry? Have you never asked yourself these questions? They are orphans from both sides.

All four of you were adopted. Okay, maybe they had just joined the family but that doesn't mean anything, son. Right is right. All four of you were adopted by your late father Hikmet and your late mother Filiz. Have you forgotten those times? I know that this must be going through your mind but there is nothing that Mrs. Nalân had not done. How many times did she take large sums of money from you while you slept and maybe you realized it, maybe you didn't but wake up. Open your eyes, my son. Look, someone sent you evidence to warn you, whoever it was, I thank him for opening your eyes. Wake up, my son. The deceased were righteous people.

This inheritance is tied to sweat and hard work but you are four children. Now you must come to your senses, not only do you have a right to this inheritance but your siblings also have a right to it. You should call them and ask for them. This is your first and foremost religious duty, then your duty as a stepbrother. According to the judicial authorities, now they can also file a criminal complaint. There are many other things, my son, I don't want to list them one by one. It's a good thing you signed a prenuptial agreement back then. No matter how many years you have been married, according to the contract you will pay the money immediately and get rid of the woman completely so that you don't have to deal with her anymore. That's it ... And whatever is in the contract, I ask that it be paid from your share. Please don't touch the rights of the children, look for them, my son, that is your religious and humanitarian duty."

Aunt Meral had a way of telling the story as if she had been there, as if she had heard and experienced the conversation live. It was as if she had really been present but my Aunt Meral had such a style without adding more or less.

"Do you talk to each other, do you talk on the phone from time to time? Do you have Yasemin's number, if so, can you give it to me? These are the questions your brother asked me. What should I say, my daughter?" my aunt Meral had asked.

"Okay, that's a good idea. He can reach me after eight o'clock until ten o'clock at night," I replied following our conversation so we closed the subject. That way, I wouldn't be surprised out of the blue when my brother suddenly called. At least I would be prepared for the call.

The person who hurts;
Fear your revenge!

CHAPTER
17

It Was Friday!

Although everything seemed a little complicated, everything was well organized, the way I wanted it to be. After I had taken care of one thing, I was going to take care of the next. One by one, I would settle up with them. This stage may not be easy for me, I had to use a lot of strength and fortitude but I had to make it in the end. There was no giving up. I would still face them all.

My brother had called me that same evening. I was excited when I saw the Turkish number on the display of my phone and the first thing that came to mind was my stepbrother Nihat. This was the opportunity to talk to my brother again after many years. He must have been upset about what Uncle Osman had said to him because he was ashamed. After a twenty-minute phone conversation, we continued the conversation via video call. He was very surprised about my change.

"Where have I been all these years?" he kept asking. It was as if my brother had fallen into a trance state after the sudden death of our father Hikmet and mother Filiz and had just awakened. Of course, when the dishonest woman next to him left, he could see everything more clearly. My aunt Meral had also told me that she had experienced this change.

Honestly, I was curious about him. On the phone, I witnessed his awakening myself.

My brother had stressed several times that we must come to Türkiye. When I said, "We want to spend our vacation in Türkiye," he was excited. He started making plans instantly. But I wanted to return immediately after a day or two, after taking my siblings to my Aunt Meral and Uncle Osman. When I said that, my brother said, "Okay, how nice! We're all together again."

That was a good development.

But I really wanted to meet Mrs. Nalân, even if it was only once. In Germany, the Easter vacations were just around the corner. On these holidays, I wanted to send my siblings to Türkiye to visit my Aunt Meral, who had not been able to fly to Türkiye since we arrived in Germany. For a day or two, I stayed with them. The excitement grew in me from day to day. The preparations for our vacation in Türkiye had begun. I did our souvenir shopping during the lunch break because time was very short and limited. I had tried to reconcile everything.

In the meantime, I had gotten permission from my employer for my vacation. Good Friday was a holiday, Easter Sunday and Easter Monday everything was closed ... But the worst thing was that on Saturday everything was open and I had to work. My colleague at work said, "It's okay, you take your vacation, go to Türkiye with your siblings, I'll come to work." Thanks to him, I was able to organize our plane tickets accordingly.

Not wanting to waste any time, I had booked our plane tickets for Thursday evening. My siblings would stay for twelve days. I wanted to stay from Thursday evening until Monday noon, which was enough for me anyway. But I was very excited for my siblings, it would be a change for them.

Although I thought that Kiraz was still young and might not remember, most of the memories from that time had stayed with her.

But I no longer had little Kiraz in front of me; we were the same size now. Imagine how much time had passed! Kiraz had been in first grade back when we had lived in my aunt's house. Today Kiraz was thirteen years old. We will celebrate her birthday in Türkiye during our vacation. Now she was already turning fourteen. It was only a year until she graduated from middle school which was unimaginable. How fast the time passed.

How could we stay as we were when time passed so quickly? Suat had become a tall, intelligent, handsome young man.

At the age of eighteen, he had finished middle school and was completing a three-year high school diploma. It was not a luxury to start studying right after graduation. He had to go through this phase, there was no other way!

As for me, I had turned twenty-four this year. Time marches on, sometimes mercifully, sometimes cruelly but it marches on inexorably. My two siblings were my honor. I felt honored by both of them.

The next few days would be very hectic for me because it was still three months until the end of my vocational training. Now I was in the middle of preparing for the exams. Most people thought the profession consisted of cutting hair. But if they knew what it meant, they wouldn't talk like that. Of course, there were those who knew its value. In the meantime, my employer informed me that she was going to enter me for a new competition in a contest that was for those who were doing vocational training. It was again for the golden scissors. She left it up to me to decide in which field I would enter the competition. After reading the rules of the contest, I told her my preferences at work: "Color, blow-dry and updo," I said. According to my wishes, she registered me for the contest.

The individual seeking his right is free!

CHAPTER
18

It was Thursday 05:15.

Today We Flew to Türkiye!

I had set the alarm clock for 04:00. With a cup of coffee I sat in the kitchen. The laundry from the evening was in the dryer and running, a machine full of laundry was just washed. Since my siblings were asleep upstairs, they were not awakened by the sound of the running machine. In this respect I was reassured because even though they were in bed, I could make my preparations for our vacation in the house as I wished.

We had brought all our suitcases downstairs in the evening. So I packed the last utensils, our flight left at 21:45. I didn't have much time because I preferred to be prepared, I was not one of those who panicked at the last minute. Of course, things were different in every situation and circumstance.

Actually, today was my school day but in Germany the schools were closed because there were vacations for the holidays. Therefore, I had to work today and my siblings' schools were also closed for the vacations. While I was at work, Kiraz and Suat went to run the last errands and buy the last souvenirs. Everything was going as it should.

After I got ready, I went to work, there the time passed very quickly. But I was also very excited because this time we would travel in a different way. Although there was a lot to do that day, my employer sent me home around five in the evening. She seemed even more worried than I was, "You won't make your flight," she kept saying. So I was able to be home on time and finish the last touches without stress.

It was incredible but we were really on the plane now. Finally, we left all the stress behind. It was very nice to reconnect with Nihat after all these years. It was a surprising but beautiful developmen that had strengthened my sense of unity and solidarity. Uncle Osman and brother Nihat would pick us up from the airport.

On Monday morning I also had an appointment with my lawyer, nicknamed bloody Nigar. Let's see how the developments affected me this time or what changes they would bring about in me. I was excited and tired, so I kept it short:

Goodbye for now!

Now I was on the plane back to Germany!

The days had passed so quickly, it was unbelievable. Today was really already Monday. My siblings would stay for another ten days. We were very well received, it was the second time I had experienced this feeling, for my siblings it was the first time.

They were longing for these feelings, the feeling of family, the affection of mom and dad, a crowded family environment. These were unknown and untried feelings for us.

My brother was very surprised when he saw us. When we were sent away at that time, all three of us had still been children. Yes, Kiraz was the youngest but considering the circumstances of her life, Kiraz didn't look thirteen at all. We had celebrated her birthday on Sunday when she had turned fourteen. I had prepared a special birthday cake. We had organized a surprise party for Kiraz in the house. She was very happy, it was Kiraz's right to be happy and have feelings of happiness.

Again I became sad that my siblings could not grow up in an environment with mom and dad. But there was no other way, it had to be that way. There had never been any room for bad habits like objection or rebellion. Praise and thanks were due to God for every condition and situation for every time and situation.

On Saturday I was able to spend quite a bit of time with my brother Nihat. We were also able to discuss very serious topics. This was very good for both Nihat and me. On this occasion I had learned many other things.

For example, that he had tried to call us several times but my aunt had always turned him away with all kinds of excuses, like "she's sleeping, she's at work, she's shopping, she has a job." While I thought that my brother had called us no more than six times, he told me that he had made more than sixty calls. I also learned that he had tried to reach us through letters, had tried to meet our financial needs and had sent us pocket money several times.

I had never received a cent also I had experienced many other things ... It was incredible.

I knew nothing about all this. This injustice that my aunt had committed was unacceptable.

He insisted on showing me all the documents such as account receipts that he had sent me money. While he continued to narrate absorbed in the files in front of me, he took out all the shipping documents and put them in front of me. My brother sent six hundred euros a month for us. He sent two hundred euros a month for each of us which we had never seen and in addition to this monthly payment, he had sent us various amounts of money from time to time for our additional needs.

For example: school trips, school expenses, seasonal clothing, furniture, vacation ..

After my brother told me these things, I was very shocked. My anger toward my aunt had increased. This was officially unfair. While we had spent three years in that coal cellar, in the darkness of the cellar, in the damp, the cold, the dirt, the rust and the mold, it had turned out that a lot had been going on behind our backs. In that conversation, I had learned something else. My aunt had never told my brother that we had moved into my aunt's apartment.

She just said, "They're going to spend the two-week vacation with their aunt. They went to their aunt's house."

With excuses like these, she kept giving false information to my brother. This woman was an outright fraud! I could not even call her aunt.

With the tips I received at the hairdressing salon where I did my internship, I was able to provide for our daily food, drinks and necessities at that time which amounted to about ten euros a day.

Sometimes I got seven euros in tips, sometimes only three euros but sometimes twelve euros. I worked four days a week in the salon and the other days I was at school. I usually did our shopping at the end of the market because the prices were lowered then. Of course, this tip was not enough to sustain us because I could not afford to buy anything else.

We had a small hand stove with gas. That was all we had for cooking our meals. While doing this, please imagine that my siblings and I had lived in that basement. Imagine that I used to light a fire in front of the garden exit door of the basement to heat the water and wash our clothes that way.

In snow, winter, rain, storm ... God only knows how I had lit the fire back then. I remembered well how we had spent those days, I knew what we had gone through. There were two washing machines upstairs in my aunt's house, although both were in operation, we did not have permission or the right to use them. I remembered how I used to wash our clothes by hand outside. The hand washing was not the problem but the whole situation. That was unfortunate!

There was no stove, no lamp, no heating. Whatever garbage there was, it was stuffed into other empty rooms. My siblings and I had lived in a place where even mice could not find shelter. We had just arrived in Germany. There was neither a language nor knowledge of travel. We had been completely harassed.

After getting some information from him, I told my brother what had happened. He was surprised and shocked by this. I had even shown him pictures from that time. He became tense and quite angry. "I will take care of it!" he rumbled.

I then asked him, "How?"

"I need to talk to her first before I take any further steps," he explained. Without wasting much time, my brother picked up the phone and called my aunt.

"There's no point in talking too long, I'm going to sue you," he said, then he had already hung up. Briefly he had told me that she had only mumbled indistinctly through the receiver. After that, without even looking at me, he immediately called his lawyer. He explained the situation as it was. If it was too late on Monday (since I would be flying back to Germany), he invited me to his home for that day. Otherwise, we would have had to make an appointment at his office on Monday with our evidence and supporting documents but this was better.

When the lawyer arrived, my brother had already copied and prepared all the evidence.

In the meantime, I said to my brother, "Mrs. Nalân had given a lot of money to my aunt at that time, almost a hundred and fifty thousand TL and then another hundred thousand TL to have me brought to Germany."

My brother could not believe what he was hearing.

"At the airport I gave your aunt five thousand euros in an envelope," he said. My aunt had told him that the upstairs was not yet finished and that she would have it fixed up for us. "Five thousand euros is enough for now," she said then. This woman was a fraud. As I learned these things little by little, my anger at her grew and grew. She wanted to renovate the upstairs for us so that my siblings and I could live well in this house. Wow! The question marks in my mind dissolved one by one. This dishonest woman was one of the revenge actions I still wanted to take. My revenge would be very bad this time.

When the lawyer had come to us, he wanted to get the truth about the matter from me. He had placed a recording assistant on the table to record the testimony. I was no stranger to this assistant at all, a device I used all the time whenever I could.

"You can file a lawsuit in Germany and I will take care of your case from here," the lawyer suggested.

That had already been my intention.

"I will send you the results and developments in this case. If I translate them into German, you will have a well-developed case with excellent evidence," the lawyer suggested. Of course, I immediately agreed. Why not?

The backgrounds were solved day by day. This, of course, gave me a good feeling of relief. The absurd thing was that my brother was still sending her six hundred euros a month. *Would you laugh or cry about this situation?* I was surprised about that too! My brother had also told me that letters had come from the prosecutor's office which he had put in another envelope without opening them. Then he had sent them to my aunt's address in Germany so that they would reach me. However, my aunt had never told me about my letters or his phone calls. So I had no information at all.

We had spent Saturday like this, it was 8:00 in the evening.

After Nihat returned all the files to his study, he said to me, "Yasemin, I really didn't know what was going on or I would have intervened earlier. Please forgive me." His words meant a lot to me.

As I had expressed several times, I did not harbor any anger or resentment toward my brother. For a while I was offended but when I saw that he was also a victim, I really wanted to help him. Because of the breakdown in communication, some unnecessary misunderstandings had arisen. We wanted to clarify that in conversations.

My brother and I had cooked the herbal tea of our uncle Osman. We sat on the terrace with a blanket and hot tea afterward, engaging in a lively and deep conversation. When he realized that I was no longer a little girl, he confided a lot in me during this conversation. In other words, it had not been easy for my brother either. Even though I was certainly not angry with my brother for what had happened, that was clear, he was plagued by feelings of guilt.

Even when we were engrossed in various topics, he would occasionally make statements like, "If I had known, I would have done something!" However, the topic was closed and we had already dealt with other issues.

Something had to happen and something did happen. Since we couldn't make up for what had happened, we couldn't bring back the past either. From now on, we just wanted to make healthier decisions about our future and be more careful so we didn't get into those situations again. That was all!

During this intense conversation it had already become 9:30 in the evening. My dearest ones had still not called. My brother called Uncle Osman. "We are on our way, son, we will be home soon," he said.

It was a great relief for me that my brother and I could solve and settle these problems without wasting time. My peace of mind was increasing day by day because the criminals would be punished.

My brother also raised another serious issue.

"What does Suat want to study? When will he finish school? When will he start his studies? What does he plan to do?"

I had asked myself the same questions, then we had discussed all the issues one by one, down to the smallest detail. My brother, just like my father, the late Mr. Hikmet, had said to my brother at that time:

"Come, my son, take your post in the holding company."

This time my brother applied this attitude to me. He had also presented good ideas for the future of Kiraz.

Thereupon I had replied: "I thank you for your good thoughts, of course also for your healthy ideas. However, it is a little difficult to realize what you are saying now. My brother Suat is in his pre- university year, he has not started his studies yet. Kiraz, on the other hand, is still in school. Although I am twenty-four years old, I am in the last months of my vocational training. My three years of vocational training will soon be over. To keep our feet firmly on the ground and become more successful, we need three or four years to realize those beautiful thoughts you mentioned."

It had not been easy for us either because I was a minor at the time when we went to Germany. *How could I intervene, how could I get out of this situation?* I could not.

It had taken us a long time to get out of this harassing situation. Now we had created a new order, a new life for ourselves. We had completely renewed everything. A new city, a new workplace, everything you could imagine was new to us. First of all, we had to establish an order. We needed to recover and we were making good progress in creating that order. We now had a neat and organized life which we did not have then.

We had started everything in a nice way, albeit with difficulties, but it was not possible to break off this labor-intensive phase halfway and walk away. We had to persevere to the end and had no intention of abandoning our goals halfway. That was the essence of the matter.

Uncle Osman, Aunt Meral, the driver and my siblings arrived home at 9:50. They all had smiles on their faces. They returned home with their hands full of bags. They also took a seat next to us on the terrace with joy. Although it was April, the evening was not chilly and cold but just in case, we still sat in that cozy family atmosphere, tucked under our blankets.

Although Aunt Meral was tired, she got up to prepare snacks. With a smile, she went to the kitchen. "So we have a long night," I laughed and I got up to help. That evening we had made it through the night by 02:45 with beautiful and deep conversations. We were celebrating Kiraz's birthday when the clock struck 00:00.

I was happy!

On Sunday after breakfast, we had visited the graves of my late mother Filiz and my late father Mr. Hikmet. It had been very sad, we had said our prayers at their graves. After watering their flowers, we had gone back home. When the time came, we would also be buried in the family cemetery. Then we would all be side by side. My uncle Osman insisted, "I will take care of their graves with my own hands, I will clean them, I will take care of them." That is why they had not assigned anyone else. May God be pleased with my uncle Osman. A man full of compassion, a man with the heart of a father!

When I was in Türkiye a few months ago, I had never mentioned that I had visited their graves. When the subject came up, it came up again.

On Monday morning, my brother had told me that he wanted to take Suat and Kiraz to the holding company. I had an appointment with my lawyer, nicknamed bloody Nigar. After my appointment, I was going to go to the holding without stopping at home first and I was going to go home first after we had lunch together which I did. My brother's lawyer had given me a copy of the criminal complaint filed with the prosecutor's office as evidence when I visited the holding. It contained all the necessary evidence. This evidence would suffice for me in Germany. As soon as I returned, I would deal with this issue.

My siblings were quite happy with their situation. This had made me happier.

My lawyer Nigar and I had dealt in detail with my stepmother whose sentence had been increased for other reasons. She was currently in prison serving her sentence. Through my lawyer, I had intended not to give her a single cent from our father's inheritance. We had a plot of land, a house made of mud, and fields in our village, but I really had no intention of letting her smell even a little of it because of this injustice she had done to my siblings and me. However, I didn't want the money either. No way! We were going to donate it as soon as we got it.

Knowing that this punishment would be even harsher for her than the prison she was in now, it would stick to her like a slap in the face. Once she had tried to sell the house and fields but since she was not the only one entitled to inherit, she could not carry out her ugly plan. Even though I had no contact, I knew everything very well.

My attorney had drafted a letter on behalf of my stepmother stating that she did not want any of the inheritance with her consent and had her sign it herself in jail. Only my lawyer could have done that. Everything that our father and mother had left now passed into the name of my siblings and me. But during my trip to Türkiye, I had no time to deal with inheritance matters.

My brother and sister came home around 2:00 in the afternoon.

That had made me very happy. We had gained time to talk a little more but those few days were definitely not enough. My brother was more emotional than I thought. He was full of need to talk more than I was. I was witnessing what I was seeing and experiencing with amazement. Some events were not what we thought. It was a reassuring situation.

So I also told my brother about my appointment with my lawyer. That's when he offered, "I can also take care of the sale, we have a lot of people, as long as you want me to."

From then on, my brother was our supporter. No, no, I had worded that sentence a little wrong. My brother was always our supporter but that was covered up by some people. I wanted to take care of those cover-ups myself. This time, my revenge was going to be dirty.

My farewell to all had been sincere, warm, and loving. The landing at the airport in Germany was imminent. The plane was preparing to land, the stewardesses were going about their duties to check that the seat belts were fastened and that each passenger was seated.

Even though the visit was short, it had been very nice. The development and realization of some events that I had never expected brightened it further. I returned to my house with a smile on my lips, I was cheerful, upright, peaceful and happy.

Taste of revenge;
It's delicious with the best justice.

CHAPTER
19

Home Again!

It was the first time I had been home without my siblings because until today they had never slept somewhere else, not even for one night. I myself had left my siblings alone for a night only once when I had gone looking for a job.

Tomorrow was another work day so I didn't want to exert myself any more today. I just unpacked my suitcase and quickly washed the clothes in the washing machine. The inside of the house was clean, I didn't need to do anything.

In the living room, I sat in front of my computer and searched the Internet for a lawyer of Turkish origin in my area. From now on, I would be able to handle my cases from there. Lawyers of Turkish origin were found on several lists of lawyers.

On Tuesday morning, before I left for work, I wanted to call off the numbers I had written down from several lawyers because there was no point in dragging this out.

Again I thought of my aunt with whom I had lived in Germany for two years. I had called her from a secret number and we had talked on the phone for almost an hour and a half. She was also going through an extraordinary development, as she was in the process of separating from her husband. As her problems grew from day to day and the feeling of "enough is enough" took hold of her, she prepared herself for the separation. She had been in the hospital continuously for eleven months. My brother-in-law, as you remember, was a truck driver. When he was at work, he was on the road between two and seven days. When he was home, he stayed three to seven days each time.

One day, when he was back home, during an argument with my aunt, he splashed the hot oil from the pan that had been on the stove into her face. From her face to her neck and almost to her shoulders she was burned.

These scars from the burns remained until her death. Her treatments were still ongoing. She had survived minor and major surgeries. I could not believe what I was hearing. How could people torture each other like that? I was amazed at that. I never had any problems with my aunt. In any case ... My brother-in-law was in prison for this crime.

He was a psychopath, he didn't have a healthy soul. I had always said that when we had lived with them. After the bad news I had heard, I wanted to see my aunt as soon as possible to be with her and support her during this difficult time. So I invited my aunt to our home. She had no one but us. She was on her own and after this tragic incident, with the help of the state, she had the opportunity to move out of the house where she lived. While she was in the hospital, the staff of the women's shelter organized this visit.

This is what I liked most in Germany, because "HUMAN RIGHTS!" came first. After this terrible situation, my aunt received moral support from some state organized officials. They accompanied her to shopping and took her to appointments. When I learned that my aunt was now a person in need of help, my heart hurt even more.

Since the day we left her house, my aunt did not know where we lived. She had no contact information from me. So it was impossible to get in touch with me! For the first time, I had given her our address and my phone number. If the situation had not been like this, I might not have given them. We had ended our phone conversation that evening with the words, "We'll be in touch."

About their situation I was very sad! I was inconsolable ... A few days later I received a call from my aunt.

"My dear, I talked to my aides, they said they could bring me to you. They were happy that I am no longer alone, that a relative had come forward. I am very embarrassed, you know I don't like to be needy but what should I do, what can I do? Which day suits you, my beautiful girl?" she asked me.

"Let's not waste any more time, I think we should talk to your aides as soon as possible to ask them to bring you here as soon as possible," I offered. "I'll get back to you when they give me a date," she said sheepishly. We said our goodbyes and then hung up the phone.

Before half an hour had passed, I received another phone call. This time my aunt said, "I hope that tomorrow, my daughter, we will leave around 2:00 in the afternoon. So I think we will arrive at your house between half past seven and eight in the evening."

I was very happy about that, that it happened so quickly. Anyway, my working hours went approximately up to that time.

The excitement was at its peak... My shift was over, my aunt had arrived, she was already at the door! So I was in a hurry to leave my workplace. It was not far from our house. I was on the road for about fifteen minutes, I wanted to hurry home as soon as possible. The people who had brought my aunt were also waiting.

But I had no idea what kind of picture I would find. I could not have guessed my aunt's new appearance, it was nothing compared to what I had suspected. I was shocked, her figure and everything else had changed. If I saw her outside,

I definitely wouldn't recognize her, she wasn't like she used to be at all. I fervently hoped that he would suffer the harshest punishment in prison for this murderous and treacherous behavior. They sentenced my brother-in-law to twenty-three years in prison. After the exciting and frantic greeting and hug at the door, I invited them all upstairs to the house. I had started the preparations after work the day before and finished the rest of the preparations that morning. The food was ready, of course, it just needed to be heated. After the helpers had satisfied their needs and had a cup of coffee, they went on their way again. We said our goodbyes after saying that we would telephone the day of my aunt's return.

I could not believe what I saw. My aunt was in a terrible condition. Her burns extended to her chest. The burned skin was incredibly covered with scars and holes. She no longer had a nose. There were only cavities down to the bone. Oh my God, it was so bad. He had abused my aunt. Through the minor and major surgeries she had to undergo, she was restored as she is now but still this condition was very scary and horrible.

At the kitchen table, my aunt began to tell me the terrible events of that day as follows: "Your brother-in-law came home after working for four days. The first thing he did was to go to the bathroom, then there was dinner, tea and so on.

The usual routine when he came home. While he was relaxing in the bathtub, I prepared the rest of the food. He called for me a few times but I didn't hear his calls. The door to the kitchen was closed because I was working at the stove. The sounds from the water and the roasting had been too loud. The window was open and the sounds from outside also penetrated the apartment. No matter how much he called, he could not be heard.

Also, he never had the habit of calling from the bathroom. He usually went in, then came out again.

"You are not in bondage to me?" he began to shout, more like screech, as soon as he entered the kitchen. How could I not hear the master? As soon as he had the rolling pin in his hand, he first quickly hit my legs.

My cries for help were in vain - don't do it, don't hit me, I didn't hear it. He continued to beat me mercilessly and furiously with the thin and long rolling pin until I fell to my knees. While I was on my knees, he also started hitting my arms and head with the rolling pin. I desperately tried to hold the rolling pin with my hands to protect myself but he violently snatched the rolling pin from my hands and hit me once or twice in the face with his fist while I was still on my knees, pulling me back by my hair.

Then unable to contain his rage, he took the pan with the hot oil from the stove, which he poured into my face. A split second, yes ... A split second that made me what I am today. What happened after that was already done. My screams and wails were useless. The neighbors, who had called the police, rescued me from this terrible and violent situation then the ambulance came, surgeries and treatments followed. Today I am here, my little one."

When I heard this in detail from my aunt, the following words of our Prophet came to my mind:

"LET HIM WHO IS IN PAIN BE PATIENT. THE ONE WHO INFLICTS PAIN SHOULD WAIT FOR THE DAY WHEN HE WILL BE HURT."

Prophet Muhammad (SAW)

It was so sad, I was very confused. What I had heard was like something out of a movie. My aunt needed a lot of love, care and understanding from now on. We all needed it at any time and in any situation but this situation was different from other situations.

Because I was afraid of my brother-in-law, I couldn't call my aunt very often. The last time I had called, my brother-in-law had answered the phone so I had hung up quickly. That day was my last call until Sunday. *But I was glad that I had called again after all!*

We had talked intensively until half past twelve at night. After I had prepared a place for my aunt to sleep, I had fallen wearily into bed but I couldn't fall asleep right away because a thousand different things were going through my mind. One example: I wanted my aunt to live with us from now on but before I could discuss this idea with my aunt, I had to get the opinion of my siblings because I felt that I was not authorized to make such a big decision on my own without their knowledge and consent. The situation was very serious. When the clock struck two in the morning, I closed my eyes and finally fell asleep.

The night was sleepless. As soon as I woke up, I started my preparations to go to work. In a hurry, I left the house after putting on clothes, hair and makeup. My aunt was still asleep. During the lunch break, I called my siblings and calmly discussed the situation with them.

When Suat heard the bad story, he immediately said, "Auntie shall stay with us from now on, sister." He made a positive impression. I quickly explained, "I wanted to talk to you about these things to get your opinion, too."

So I wanted to talk to my aunt about my plan which we had all agreed to. After my shift that night, I was going to explain this decision and our idea to her over dinner. She should no longer be alone and lonely.

We had just moved in, we had to learn everything and everywhere from scratch. We could do everything together. As long as the will was there, everything could be overcome. When I came home after my shift, my aunt had cooked and set the table. To be honest, I wasn't used to that at all, I meant because of my siblings, yes, but having my aunt with us was different. It was a nice feeling. Immediately I walked up to her and hugged her gently because her wounds were not completely healed. My heart ached when I saw her in this condition.

This was a deep wound that will not heal!

To get rid of the hair and lint left over from work, I first had to go to the bathroom and freshen up before sitting down at the table. After work, I always did it that way. After almost twenty minutes, I was back in the kitchen. "Thank you, for everything," I said to my aunt then we sat down at the table.

While we ate, I impatiently told her about our decision. Very confused, my aunt asked, "But ... But how can that be?"

"We can overcome anything as long as there is a will," I answered her. However, she said, "What about my treatments?"

"Auntie," I replied, as if to allay her fears "This is a big city, in the city where we used to live, you may have had the problem of the shortage of doctors but here there is no such problem. Here, all the specialists are available to you. You just have to ask for it."

But first she wanted to talk to the helpers that the state had given my aunt for that period. Above all, she wanted to think about it but she was not negative. She looked embarrassed. Our house was spacious, even if we hadn't had one, we would still have found a place. That could not have been the problem.

My aunt stayed with us for a week. My siblings would not return to Germany for three days so they did not meet. Their vacation was almost over. They were constantly sending me pictures.

I had not mentioned the result of my search for a lawyer of Turkish origin. Within a week I was able to make an appointment with a lawyer. At the appointment, I had presented the lawyer with all the evidence and proof about my maternal aunt. I had explained everything in great detail, as completely as I could. Our first appointment lasted almost two hours. The lawyer told me that I could sue not only for fraud but also for many other things.

He mentioned some paragraphs about human rights. To that end, he pointed out that there were various penalties for being forced to live inhumanely in the basement. Apart from the financial lawsuits that I would file, he indicated that these other problems could lead to imprisonment.

"Good, then let's file our lawsuit without interruption," I said to my lawyer as I signed my power of attorney. As the lawyer was calculating the financial aspects, he looked up and said, "That's a good idea.

Well, it's time for justice, let's see how one hundred and sixty-two thousand eight hundred and fifty euros can be squandered on the backs of half and full orphans."

The lawyer had hair on his teeth   *We would have many more collaborations with this lawyer,* I said in my heart at that moment. May God bless him. After we shook hands and I said goodbye, I made my way to my workplace with my head held high.

That day, my aunt's lawyer told her that he would prepare the letter and at the same time report the other crimes to the prosecutor's office. From now on, it was just a matter of waiting. I wanted to take revenge on all of them, one way or another!

While my other aunt was still living with us, my lawyer sent me copies of the letters he had sent to the prosecutor's office. "Wow, well done! How well he put it," I said after reading them, then I put the letters in my files.

I did not want to tell my aunt about this matter. I didn't want to bother her with these things, since she was already struggling with her own problems. Everything had its time and place. One day she would hear it from me but now was not the time.

The developments were extraordinary. After my aunt left, I called my brother Nihat and informed him about the meeting with the lawyer. He was very pleased with the news. "Justice must be done, God willing" he said. Neither my brother Nihat in Türkiye nor I in Germany wanted to give up these cases. There was strength and power in unity.

Justice surely triumphs in the end.

CHAPTER
20

The next three days I was still alone at home.

In the meantime, I would be able to continue my recordings without interruption. It was long past time to turn my attention to the exams of my profession. I had to pass the exam because I didn't want to have to retake it. To pass, I had to study for my exam. I had to be strong and ready for both the theoretical and practical exams. The rest of the problems were not going to come to the fore until after the exam. There were still three months until the exam.

Before our vacation in Türkiye, I had mentioned that my employer had signed me up for the *GOLDEN SHERRY* contest which was in two and a half weeks. I had to put a lot of effort into that. It was a nice feeling to have won second place in my first participation in the competition. I felt honored. It was exciting and there had been personal development. Especially for my self-confidence because in my eyes it was a success.

NO, NO ... It was not about arrogance!

With humility, you will be even more eager to learn! But before I digressed further, I wanted to say that the competition came at the wrong time. We had overcome most things, I would overcome this too, God willing.

Lately, everything had been moving a little too fast. I had to continue at this pace until the exams. I hoped that I would have a few quiet and stress-free days after the exams.

The time passed quickly. Luckily I was together with my siblings again!

I had picked them up from the airport in a cab. They came back with full suitcases and they were tanned. When I saw them like that, I wanted to bite them. I had missed my siblings very much. Now they were both in bed, I was sitting in my room. My siblings were everything to me, may God never snatch them away. I didn't know what I would do if they were gone! When they were both home, I had prepared our meals accordingly, like Kiraz liked this and Suat liked that. We had planned our days accordingly. While they were away, I had asked myself what to cook, "So, what do you like?"

Unfortunately, I could not answer this question. Suddenly I froze, while my thoughts were in completely different places, *where were they? Where had I suddenly flown with my thoughts?* I had set sail with my thoughts, into a life I didn't know, into *MY OWN LIFE* that I had never lived. While I was immersed in a completely different world with my thoughts, I fell asleep on my bed. My siblings had to go back to school the next day without even a day of rest at home. Their school vacation was over. They will be a little tired but they were no longer little.

No matter, I still could not do without them!

Again I had received a letter from the lawyer because of my aunt! But I was in shock, it was unbelievable! This woman was dishonest, deceitful, corrupt, vicious, every bad habit and behavior imaginable was present in this woman. She could also be called a fox. *What would happen?* I was so tense, I had to pull myself together! She should give an account before my Lord, I wished her love for God and deep faith. You could deny everything but not to this extent and not before God!

Justice will be served, I said confidently and emphatically. Justice will be done, no one could doubt that.

The day after this letter, the public prosecutor's office issued a warrant for my aunt's arrest, and according to the criminal complaint I had filed through my lawyer, she had to appear before a judge. This news had hit me hard, I never expected it to happen so quickly. The whole time I had to swallow. With the letter in my hand, I ran from one side to the other and was stunned!

Exactly one day later, I also received a letter from the prosecutor's office. *"God, what is this? I hope it's something good,"* I said. It was an appointment, an invitation to the prosecutor's office in the city where I lived at the time. There I was to give my testimony. Now I had to talk about those nightmarish days in front of the judge. But I don't want to remember those days. I was so affected that I had become a person who was afraid of the dark. It had really been three terrible years. It was like a horror movie. Only those who live like rats in basements know that.

When I remembered those days again, this came to mind: Imagine motor oil. We lived in such a liquid, oily substance in the dirt. Most of the walls were smeared with this black oil. Since it was mostly dark in the basement, we had to feel our way around these oily walls because we couldn't see anything. There was also rust and other dirt, it was a coal cellar where we had lived. There was another door in the corridor that was just slightly ajar; but they had fixed it with concrete. Whatever idiot did that! There was maybe a meter of space behind the door. There were a lot of cables there.

When it had become light outside, a little light had penetrated inside. When we opened the cellar door that led to the garden, it became a little brighter. Otherwise it was dark. *And what did we do when it got dark?*

Yes, what had we done? We had a lamp that illuminated the corridor a little. That was if we had electricity. There was a power cable that was run from the top floor. On a whim, they plugged in and unplugged the power. On a whim they would just unplug it, this woman I called my aunt was cruel. Sometimes I would go upstairs and ask her to plug the power cord back into the outlet, to which she would give me a stroppy response and send me back downstairs, sometimes she would even chase me away. This was very annoying.

After a few such experiences, I bought battery-powered lamps with my leftover tip money. My siblings couldn't do their homework. I couldn't cook, we couldn't see, it was too dark.

Especially in the winter days, oh my Lord, oh my beautiful Lord Almighty, those were bad days. May God help me, I never wanted those days to happen again. For no one! (Amen)

Don't be a life-darkener, be a lifesaver.

Yasemin's Struggle

CHAPTER
21

On The Train Again!

Finally, I had my full testimony in the presence of the judge at the prosecutor's office behind me. Now I returned home feeling lighter, full of peace. There was no way to describe what a nice feeling it was. Justice is being served. It has always been that way and will remain that way.

Tomorrow was the *GOLDEN SCISSORS* competition. I was thrilled at how quickly two and a half weeks had passed, the time flew by.

Two days ago I had another heartbreaking incident. It had been evening time. My two siblings had gone to their rooms to sleep. But I was still preparing my model's hair for the contest. After an hour and a half, my model had left. Afterwards, I had cleaned up a bit.

After taking the laundry out of the dryer and folding it, I went upstairs quietly to put the folded laundry in my siblings' living room. From Kiraz's room, I heard sounds like she was crying. Yes, Kiraz had been crying in her room. Quietly, I had approached the door which was one of my unloved habits. It was a disregard for privacy, I was also very angry with myself but Kiraz was my little mouse, when I had heard her crying I couldn't help it.

I can't spare a single tear from her. Suddenly, I heard Kiraz's soft sobs, "Mommy, Mommy, Mommy." At that moment my hair stood on end, my eyes were bloodshot. I quickly left the room quietly so Kiraz wouldn't notice me and had gone back downstairs! Again, I went up to the second floor with another load of laundry but this time I made deliberate noises.

While I was sorting my siblings' laundry in the living room, Kiraz carefully opened the door. "Sister!" she whispered. Immediately, I stood up. "Aren't you asleep, my little mouse?", I asked, then hugged her warmly. Her head was resting on my chest. She hugged me tightly and closed her eyes.

"Are you okay, sweet mouse?", I echoed. "I'm fine, sister. Thank God I'm fine!" she replied in a slightly tired and tearful voice. Her head was still resting on my upper body and she was holding me with her arms around me. I caringly stroked her hair.

"Come on, spit it out, sweet witch," I urged her very sincerely. Without taking a breath, she asked me, "What was my mother like?" At that moment I got a slap but of course I hadn't let on. Since I had heard her cry before, this subject was a very delicate one. She had done what she had done to me.

Yes, this woman was the mother of my Kiraz. Because of my infinite love and respect for Kiraz, of course I should not badmouth her as if I were angry with her or spreading hate and hatred. But unfortunately I had these thoughts for this woman.

How else could I describe such an unscrupulous woman? For a while I left the question like that in the room, then without lifting my head I said, "Enough to go to jail." She then hugged me tightly.

Kiraz had been crying, I was crying because Kiraz was crying. Of course, we didn't burst into tears, we cried quietly, as if we were shedding tears of sorrow after a sad loss.

When Suat heard us, he came out of his room and entered the living room in a daze.

"What's going on with you, is there bad news?" he asked, clearing the table a little. I was very happy about the distraction because I had unexpectedly gotten into this situation. I wish I could have said two or three nice sentences about my stepmother Kiraz's birth mother to comfort Kiraz a little bit in this emotional moment. But unfortunately, I couldn't think of a good sentence at that moment. I couldn't even say a nice word to comfort her, unfortunately.

After Suat came in, we had not talked about the subject.

As the two of them made their way back to their rooms, I called after Kiraz, "Kiraz, maybe I wasn't ready for the questions you just asked me. It went unanswered, suddenly I didn't know what to do. This is a very sensitive issue, I didn't approach your problem professionally. Maybe at that moment I should have said two sweet sentences to you and then sent you to bed. BUT ... That would not be right! In my opinion, it is your natural right to know everything as it is. Let's discuss this issue later like two mature people. Let's go down to the smallest detail, to the bottom of the matter. I am ready to talk about it with you and Suat."

Suat had understood what was going on after what I had said.

It was as if a difficult time had begun, like a new stage in our lives. Only I know how many times I had prayed in my heart that we would put this time behind us as soon as possible and that everything would be okay again. There was no other way out!

Yes, that's it for the developments. Goodbye for now!

In the meantime I had received a letter from my lawyer, my aunt was imprisoned for four years and six months. Now it was my aunt's turn to see the inside of the prison. My brother-in-law and my two cousins were fined. Each of my cousins had been fined thirteen thousand euros for looking the other way and violating human rights in this crime. My brother-in-law was even fined thirty-thousand euros when it was discovered that he was the head of the snake in the criminal organization.

Do not take the favor of the victim, it will take revenge in the end!

"Let them taste what it means to abuse the rights of orphans," my lawyer had said. Honestly, I didn't expect them to be punished to this extent. I thought that I could at least make my claim for the monthly money my brother had sent me but it turned out that letting my siblings and me live in such a situation for years was a criminal act.

My lawyer demanded everything back, from the monthly money my brother had sent my aunt to the monthly child support we had received from the state. He gave them fourteen days to pay the amount of two hundred and seventeen thousand eight hundred and fifty euros mentioned in his letter. Let's see ...

However, I knew that they will not be able to pay ... Above all, they will also not be able to pay the fines they had received. That was the point, they couldn't pay! If I had to, I had everything confiscated from them, I plucked them to the feathers. Money didn't matter to me, it wasn't about money! This injustice, this cruelty that was done to us had to be punished. Did they think that the Lord Almighty had no scales? If not in this world, justice will be done in the hereafter.

Of course, when I learned some of the facts through my brother, I rudely said, "What a bad woman.

While we went shopping from the market in supply time with the money I earned from my tips, like patches we sewed on our clothes or clothes others threw away, she lived in prosperity. The six hundred euros we had received every month from my brother, plus the four hundred and sixty-two euros from the state, the child support for the three of us my aunt kept for herself. We had never seen a cent of that money, God was our witness! Even the child benefit from the state would have helped us a lot. Even if it would not have been enough for three heads, but still. But with this money she had to pay the rent for the coal house. She was such a woman!

In the next period, apart from work and my siblings, I spent the rest of my time just worrying about my exam. There was very little time left until then. But I had no intention of retaking it. I had to pass no matter what, I had to study for it.

In addition, there was the GOLDEN SCISSORS contest, in which I had done the updo on my model. In fact, I had won it and received the GOLDEN SCISSORS Award, what an honorable feeling. I don't know why but everything had turned out perfectly. When I was presented with the award, my legs had been shaking with excitement and joy. My employer had told me how honored she was. However, I didn't want to show myself in the newspapers that much so I always posed so that my face was hidden. Later, my award was displayed among the other awards in the hair salon where I worked.

Over the weekend I had a long conversation with my aunt on the phone. I told her how much my siblings and I wanted her to move in with us, whereupon she had spoken to the caregivers provided by the state.

To our relief, they had replied, "No problem, our institution is represented throughout Germany. We will forward the information about your move and your file to the organization in your new city. They will get in touch with you. You don't have to worry about anything. We will be there for you as long as you need help."

That was great. So there was no obstacle at all for our aunt to move in with us. Of course she was a little excited, in fact I thought she was a little too excited. Then she announced her decision to us, "Fine by me." She had changed her mind, she wanted to live with us too. But first she wanted to get her house fixed up which would be ready in three months. Let's go. Because of these positive developments, I experienced extraordinary happiness and peace. I had never experienced such positive and peaceful days in a row in my life. These successive good developments were new to me.

Life is as clear as a drop of water,
as dirty as a piece of mud...

CHAPTER
22

Happy News, I Passed the Exam ... Thank God!

I had worked hard for that. In my private time, I didn't have the luxury of occupying my mind with other things. I had concentrated solely on this matter. Once there had been a court hearing about my aunt that I had to attend. It had been a long train ride, this time I had forgotten to take my admissions assistant with me. Yet I had so much to tell.

In the meantime, my aunt had been living with us for two weeks. We cleared out my siblings' living room and set up a room for her. She brought her own furniture which we had set up. The rest she was either going to sell or throw away. We did our best to put her to rest.

My aunt insisted that she wanted to do some task, the hallway and the entrance of the house and the surrounding area she wanted to keep clean. Her intention was to relieve me but I was already used to this pace ...

However, my aunt said, "I feel good, I can work. Why shouldn't I contribute?" I didn't want it because her wounds were still fresh and she was still undergoing treatment but my aunt insisted. So we didn't put any obstacles in her way either because this was her home too.

One hand washed the other. In unity lay strength!

To be a woman; to be a born warrior.

Yasemin's Struggle

CHAPTER
23

In the meantime, my aunt had been living with us for six months. The time had flown by. Many things had changed in our personal lives. Each of us had gotten used to the new city we lived in. We had learned day by day what was where. This phase was very time consuming. This was a big city and even though it was a bit confusing, we had nothing to do with the whole city anyway.

My aunt received her treatments without interruption. Another surgery went smoothly. She was doing well, thank God! In the meantime, my aunt had also taken over the cleaning in the hair salon on the first floor where I cleaned. Sometimes, if it was a weekend, I had helped her. As far as possible, we had taken over all the responsibilities. It was a big change for us when my aunt had moved in with us. We had received from her the warmth that we had never experienced. We, the three siblings, felt that she completed what we had been missing. She was like a mother to us.

Suat's study preparation time was in full swing. His studies will end in a year so he had virtually no free time. Kiraz is focusing on choosing a foreign language. My employer was constantly registering us to participate in competitions. Lately, I had been thinking a lot about *enrolling in a master school.* Maybe this possibility existed for me. Let's see what happened, may God give the best, may He not embarrass any of us.

During those six months, of course, there had been some developments. My lawyer, nicknamed bloody Nigar, who also had hair on her teeth, visited my imprisoned stepmother in jail about our inheritance matters and confirmed with her signature that she had rejected her inheritance from my father and mother. During this visit, my stepmother had repeatedly slapped her knees, Nigar told me. "I am guilty, not Yasemin! She is both mother and father to my children," she had cried.

Well, in prison she had time to think. As long as she carried these thoughts in her heart, I wished her constant guidance from my Lord, hoping that in time she would purify herself of her evil feelings and thoughts and perhaps repent.

About the family to whom I was sold as a wife by my stepmother at the age of thirteen, my lawyer told me the following: "Most of them were released, the brother who drove the car and another man are still in prison. Everyone else had their sentences commuted to money."

Since I was in contact with the neighbor's daughter, I had received a lot of information from her as well. There were not many people who came and went. Before these processes had started, Leyla had left the house. From that day until now, her whereabouts were unknown. I had been happy for her.

There is a saying in Turkish "Don't laugh at your neighbor, it may happen to you" that fit this very well. Because the same thing happened to them.

Again and again she had objected, but in vain! What had happened, had happened. Above all, when an orphan is slandered, the standard of my Almighty Lord is very just. My Lord has imposed a test on them and given them a good opportunity to come to their senses. Thus, they can repent and purify themselves.

How absurd is already the word "KUMA", how bad, how stupid it is to experience such things in these times. Kuma meant second wife that should not be normal. There should be only one wife by a man's side.

The news I had received brought me further relief. My inner peace was growing day by day. The smiles we had always longed for now appeared more and more on our faces. We had a normal, organized, regular life. Work, school, private life, etc. ...

Now I had reached the end of volume eleven.

In such a short time, Yasemin had accomplished a lot, it had all happened quickly, she took one revenge after another but she did it the right way. It was the right way to take legal action!

Fortunately, what I had feared had not come to pass. For I had imagined the worst possibilities.

I was very happy that her aunt had moved in with them but also very sad that such an incident had happened to her. How cruel people can be.

A quick summary: The cassettes from twelve to fifteen had arrived at my house about two weeks ago. This time she had sent them in a small package. Since I was at work, I couldn't pick up the package from the post office until later. She had sent along cookies, candy, chocolate and a picture of her with her siblings and her aunt. On the back of the picture was written, "We are thinking of you and carrying you in our hearts!"

The records were coming in longer and longer intervals.

The best part of our work was that she was no longer crying! Yes, Yasemin was no longer desperate and had overcome her struggle. This had not escaped my notice. She had left her nightmare days behind. Yasemin was able to live a neat and organized life with her siblings. Let's take a look at the other cassettes and see what else Yasemin will tell us ...

In the eyes of a woman,
a whole world is hidden!

CHAPTER
24

Hooray! Hooray!

In three weeks, my brother came to Germany for the fair.

That was exactly what I needed now, to support each other with love, with a sense of unity and solidarity. I didn't want anything else. My brother had always said that he wanted to support me financially. Fortunately, we didn't need financial support. We were self-sufficient, thank God.

By the way, I had decided that I wanted to enroll in a master school! I had already requested the applications for enrollment and talked to my employer about it. She said she would be honored to have a master in her salon. My employer was a successful, very nice lady. She also offered that she would support me in this matter that she would not leave me alone during this time. Saying these things made me feel very good. I thanked her. Together with my employer, I had filled out the registration form and sent it by mail.

"I will single-handedly prepare you for master school, I hope it will be to your advantage," she said. The registration form indicated a few different preferences for class times.

Either only on Mondays, which would take a full year and three months. Or an additional half day a week, which would be eight months. There were two other options: a full-day, which would take five months, and the one I chose was to attend master school for three hours every evening which would take six months. That cost a lot of money. It cost eleven thousand five hundred euros.

Busy days awaited me again. The support of my aunt at home made it easier for me and my siblings. Of course, when the tasks and responsibilities we had all taken on together were fulfilled, there was no stopping us and we used up our strength to continue on our way.

My employer had been talking a lot about her mother's hairdressing salon in the last few months because she was worried. "She's old, she can't do things the way she used to, everything is always hard for her," she voiced her thoughts. "As long as I am with her, I will help her." Finally, she did not agree that her mother's hair salon should be closed.

This topic has been on the agenda more and more lately. "What if she can't make it anymore, what if it has to be closed?" she kept mentioning. It was a good, beautiful and very busy salon. Along with me, she had eight employees, so there were nine of us. She would not accept unprofessional employees. If you remember, I had worked one day a week in her mother's hair salon and that day was deducted from the rent.

Miracles come before sunrise.

CHAPTER
25

Time passed so quickly, almost three months had passed since my registration ...

I was amazed at that ... How quickly time passed. My brother had traveled to Germany. He also came to our home and was our guest. All together we helped and supported him at the booth of the fair. We all came together like a fist and said goodbye to my brother when his time was up.

The next year and a half will be very busy. It was Suat's last year at university but it was also a very important year for Kiraz. In order for her last report card to shine, she had to sit down and not lift her head from her homework and books. Because this last report card would decide her future. Where she would go would depend on her final report card. God willing!

It went on for me as well because I was accepted at the Master School. The notification of my acceptance came weeks ago by letter. There were still two months ahead of me before school started. Exhausting days were waiting for all of us. My aunt was in the hospital, they were making minor corrections to her face. I hoped and prayed that she would recover in time. Those burns on her face, neck and shoulders were going to leave scars on her body until she died. We all had to accept this fact.

By the way, I had never brought up a subject until today. Since I had just talked about my aunt, I would like to bring up this topic that had remained open. I was now immersed in the time when we had lived with my aunt, my thoughts were stuck in that time.

If you remembered, I was sexually harassed several times by my brother-in-law. When I complained, he was released from detention after three days because I had no witnesses. I had no evidence or proof of his harassment. Only the marks on my body were witnesses. These were the scars I had received when I was molested. When I had suffered a seizure at the police station and was taken to the hospital, the doctor had written out a report about my assault marks.

My brother-in-law was currently in prison for the attack on my aunt. Through my lawyer, I had requested my medical reports from the hospital. After receiving them, I made another statement to the police about the harassment by my brother-in-law from that time. My statement was taken again by the police officers and checked against my statement from years ago. They had to do that, which was fine with me because what I had said had been the truth. I had hoped that he would get another punishment on top of the one he had already received. From now on, I would have the matter handled through my lawyer.

In the last few days I have been very tired and had an extraordinary burden to carry. Throughout the day, I felt like I needed to lie down, even though I had never done so until today. The tiredness stemmed from my efforts, such as sorting out all these things in order and making sure that the criminals received their punishment. It wasn't always the same pace and even when I did make progress, everything I had hoped for didn't always happen. Body and mind needed to rest and renew. I had accomplished many things with God's permission, thank God. Most of it was over but a little remained, patience Yasemin, I said to myself.

If every night has a morning,
every ordeal must have an end...

Yasemin's Struggle

CHAPTER
26

It Was Tuesday

Almost a year had passed. We were approaching Easter again. Like last year, I wanted to fly to Türkiye again with my siblings and return before them. This time, one of the things I wanted to do on my trip was to beautify the graves of my birth parents of my mother and father. I was determined ...

So, years later, I returned to our village from which we had been expelled. In the meantime, my brother was able to sell our land and house. We had donated the money we had received from the inheritance, as we had intended.

However, I had no intention of going to our village alone. After everything that had happened, they would not let me go alone. It was thanks to them that we had all embarked on this journey together.

My aunt Meral, uncle Osman, the driver, my brother, my siblings and me. We had all joined together and traveled to our village to lay the graves of my late mother and father. First, we picked out the gravestone in our town, then we quietly drove to the cemetery.

On the way there, I remembered the nightmarish days after my father's death. At that time I was a child, about thirteen or fourteen years old. Looking at Kiraz in the car at that moment, I was lost in my dreams. *Why Kiraz?* Because my age at that time was a year or two younger than Kiraz's current age. Kiraz had turned sixteen a few days ago ... As for me, years ago, when I was fourteen, my stepmother had left me alone with my siblings whom I had never seen before, when I had returned to my father's house to make preparations for the funeral service for him in our village house. When I was a child, I experienced extraordinarily terrible days because of the slander. The villagers even broke the windows of the house.

It was incredible!

I remembered that even the gendarmerie had to stand guard at our door for a few days for protection. Unspeakably severe accusations, insults and slander came out of the mouths of individual villagers. Imagine, as a child, I was as tall as a leg. In what despair I was and what a struggle I had to fight. Especially the day we had to leave our village. Oh my God ... It was terrible. My siblings and I were almost victims of an ignorant society. From our village, a dirt road led to the main road. On this road we were not spared insults and curses.

All this had begun with my stepmother's slander against me. She had sold me to a family for money. She also slandered me by saying, "She ran away, she ran to that man." But it was not so. With her false slanders, she was now in prison I   hoped that she had come to her senses when she got down on her knees and kept whining, "What have I done?"

When some of the villagers saw a strange car, they rushed to the cemetery. We were bombarded with questions like, "Who are you, where are you from?" To which my brother replied, "We are their relatives." So he quickly ended the barrage of questions.

We also had an imam come from the city. After praying at their graves, Kiraz, Aunt Meral, me and the driver decided to go back home. The villagers had literally flocked to the cemetery asking questions. They had taken away my peace of mind years ago, at this important moment, I said, "Finally, thank God, I can dig the graves of my late mother and father. Thank God."

I had no intention of letting the villagers demoralize me again. Therefore, we thought it was right to go back immediately. As things were, I took a handful of earth from their graves to put in my bag. My brother and Uncle Osman wanted to stay so I said goodbye to them.

After all these years, I had also experienced the joy of returning to my village. But the negativity had displaced the little joy

I had experienced. They had stifled all my enthusiasm. In the evening I received a call from my brother.

"We will not return today. The graves are not ready yet! We will spend the night in a hotel in the city. I will let you know as soon as the tombs are ready," he informed me. Thank you to everyone who had contributed. I was relieved. It was a real relief for me that my mother and father now had real graves that we could visit.

Two days later I flew back to Germany.

When I was only fifteen years old, my brother had given me a thick envelope of money at passport control the day we were sent to Germany to live with my aunt.

God was my witness, I had not counted them until today. Once I had taken money out of the envelope because I had to, but after I had saved, I had put the amount back into the envelope.

Now I had brought the envelope with me. I would return tomorrow, I wanted to give him back the envelope before I flew to Germany.

The time came and my stepbrother was back home.

When the opportunity I had been waiting for presented itself, I quietly handed the envelope to my brother, who was walking around part of the terrace during the conversation: "Brother, we had a relic of yours with us, I want to return it to you," I said.

When he saw me hand him an envelope, he looked at me with an expression as if to say, *"What's wrong, what is it?"* At that moment I said, "Take it!" So I handed him the envelope again. He took it in his hand and turned his head back to me with a surprised look on his face, "Oh man, what is this now?" He opened the envelope.

When he saw that there was a bundle of money inside, he raised his voice in amazement and a little surprise:

"Yasemin? What is this now? What is this money?"

I could tell he was offended. Without going over his head, I tilted my head slightly forward and stood in front of him.

"I didn't need money then, dear brother, and I don't need it now. All I need is a family for my siblings and me. Therefore, I want you to be a family for us, to have a trunk and to be its branches. Let us grow according to the season, let us bear fruit when necessary. We are not related by blood but with the holy love that our late mother Filiz and our late father Hikmet gave us, let us be good, beautiful children to them. They deserved these things. They were people who strived for the good and faith and they provided us with the good. After all the bad days we had experienced, this place and our acceptance here, the loving welcome of my two siblings, our deep wounds had found salve. We are in a world of trials, we are in the end times Humanity is getting worse, humanity is getting terribly bad. Human beings are becoming more and more murderous as time goes on. May God forgive us all. May He protect us from evil. You have no mother and we have no father. The four of us, you, Suat, Kiraz and I, we were adopted by our late mother Filiz and our late father Hikmet who left this world and entrusted their lives to us. I just want you to be a family to us, not your money!"

My brother had listened with his head down, he was thoughtful. He had not interrupted me. It was very good that I could witness this moment. My brother understood the situation. When I finished speaking, he first grabbed my shoulder with one hand, smiled, tilted his head slightly to the side and pulled me to him to hug me. He took a deep breath and hugged me. Then, without saying a word, with his hand on my shoulder, we walked from the terrace to the living room.

"I am your brother, I hope I will always be your brother! I have three siblings, you are my family," he said solemnly.

When we entered the house, my uncle Osman had prepared his famous herbal tea and was coming towards us. What a dear person Uncle Osman was! It was the same with my Aunt Meral. May God be pleased with them. When I saw Uncle Osman coming towards us with such a tray, I honestly thought that this would not suit me. However, for them this was a normal situation. Of course; maybe it was! But I snatched the tray from his hand.

"That's enough, take a breather. You haven't rested at all today, come on, go to your seats," I urged them, holding the tray in one hand and trying to push them both into the living room with the other. After they both took their seats, I pulled a small coffee table next to them. I placed the tray on it and filled the porcelain cups with tea.

After gathering my Aunt Meral and my siblings, we all sat down in our seats. Then my brother said, "Come on, let's watch a good movie together, what do you think?"

That was a good idea, Kiraz and Suat replied, "Then let's set the table," and retreated to the kitchen.

We were going to have a movie night with the family so we had called the driver to get him involved. When he came to us, we had a full cast.

It was the last evening I would spend before returning to Germany!

Inside I was full of peace, I was with my loved ones, and I would fly to Germany tomorrow without a care in the world. What a beautiful, peaceful feeling that was, I wouldn't change it for the world. Do you think there is anything as sacred and beautiful as family? But none of us came from such a family, yes, it was my own family that was behind all the bad and negative that I had experienced. Would people with a healthy psyche ever torture a small child? I think people like that need to realize what they have done and get treatment. We had become a lynching society. Humanity was getting worse and worse ...

Now I will stop and snuggled under my comforter to sleep. It was 02:23. We had had a very nice evening tonight. It was as if warm, comforting peace resided within me. So refreshing. May the morning be good ... Good night to all of you.

And as the sun sets, new hopes arise.

CHAPTER
27

Back in Germany, I immediately went back to work. A week had already passed. It was Sunday, I was sitting quietly at the dining table in the kitchen with a cup of coffee, watching TV. I had already woken up early, it was 06:43 in the morning, so I thought I would continue where I had left off.

My brother had become the brother I had first met. That is, he was back to the way he was before he married the famous woman Nalân. My brother was back to his old self. It was as if he had been shaken up ... He had recovered, thank God!

Aunt Meral had complained about her knees this time, she had gone to the doctor but she was still in pain. So I advised her to go again, this I also told my brother to take her to a specialist.

Yes, I had left my family behind in Türkiye ... I was back in Germany.

Tomorrow my master school began. For the first time, I would attend a three-hour class after work. They had invited the newly enrolled students to the school. There they first explained to us how the process would work and what would happen in a hall in front of all the guests. It was a new step, a new beginning for me ... The excitement was at its peak.

I knew in advance that I had to make an effort. I was even afraid of writing because I was born and raised in Türkiye, *maybe a German word I didn't know would appear in the questions and therefore I wouldn't be able to answer,* such thoughts were constantly running through my head.

I had discussed these fears with my employer: "In such a case, ask your lecturers immediately, what is that word? You have to ask what you don't know so that you can answer!"

Of course, I knew in advance that the exams for the Master's certificate would be extremely difficult and exhausting. But I should also not forget what I had achieved. For myself, I said hats off.

Perhaps I could not intervene in time in all that had happened, but I had not lost myself in the face of all the atrocities, evil and calamity.

I had struggled... Yes, I had struggled!

And I had won in my battle, I had attained peace. Although I had been subjected to persecution that I did not deserve, I had not lost my faith in God despite all the torment I had experienced. During that time I had never been rebellious nor do I want to become one.

After all the negative experiences I had, I realized something!

Talking comforts, clarifies, solves ... Yes, talking had made me who I was today. I was no longer the poor, helpless Yasemin who was mute, who had to play the stubborn one. As I spoke, I realized what I had been through. I was able to solve the problems that were nagging in my head with question marks more easily by talking. It was a balm to myself. So you can read my words that were penned by the writer Nurgül.

That was life! Sometimes it was very strange ...

While I was talking about it, I was suddenly lost in the depths. My aunt was still asleep ...

Today I will have another busy day. The work in the garden came a little too short. My aunt and I had talked yesterday about today's program. At the television I had then fallen asleep. My aunt had simply ironed until 02:20 at night, because she did not want to postpone it to today. She was also feeling better in the last few days. We always divide our work. There has not been one problem between us. There has never been a problem that one of us had done more or less than the other ...

One hand washes the other, that was my general attitude. That's the only way people can complement each other. I was almost out of coffee, my aunt would wake up soon. Since I had to concentrate on starting master school, I decided not to do any audio recording for a week. Perhaps as a precaution,

I would not make any more voice recordings for the next six months. I didn't know. We would see ... I left it to my feeling!

Goodbye for now!

Today exactly one week had passed.

On Sunday morning, watching TV in the kitchen with a cup of coffee, I took another shot. A week had passed quickly again.

My prediction had been confirmed. There were difficult and exhausting days ahead of me. After work, I was in a hurry to get to school. After I started school, my work hours and my employment contract had changed. We had reduced my weekly hours. At 6:00 p.m., the work day was over. My monthly salary would not be as high as before for a while. It didn't matter ...

That was not a problem, we would get along fine for a while.

By the way, I had forgotten to say that. My siblings' vacation had already ended and they had returned home safe. Thank God, everyone was back to their tasks and duties.

This year it would be very quiet in the house because we had to study for our exams. For Suat, too, it was the last vacation in the middle of the year. His final exams started in six months but changes were coming for Kiraz as well. Suat had attended a few universities in the nearest cities in our area. His goal was to become a media and information services specialist. After his studies, he wanted to work in the holding company.

In the meantime, we had applied for German citizenship. Obtaining the necessary documents was no problem. Since we lived in a disciplined and bureaucratic country, the first thing I had to learn was to keep my paperwork neat and orderly. Everything was neatly and orderly placed in the folders.

We were able to put together what we needed in a couple of days. After we had gathered everything, we handed it in to the immigration office by hand. After we had made our last signatures, it was only a matter of time.

Now I was approaching the end of my cassette ... Once again I will stay away from my recordings for a while, because I want to dedicate myself with a clear head, to my work, my school and my family. May God make it easier for all of us.

*If you see a woman who is thoughtful and
has deep lines on her face, know that;
he's left alone with what he's been through in the past!*

Yasemin's Struggle

CHAPTER
28

Two years had passed ... How fast! Time flew by, we didn't even notice. While we were drowning in so many obligations and the daily hustle and bustle, we didn't notice how quickly time passed.

Exactly in one month, we had been living in this house for six years. For a moment, I got lost in my dreams. I hadn't done any voice recordings in the last two years. Today I had started again for the first time. Of course, a lot had accumulated that I would like to tell bit by bit. Many, many things had changed in our lives.

Let me pick up where I left off so we don't get confused.

I went to master school, my brother had been looking for a university. When I received the news from Stuttgart that my brother had been accepted to the university, I was overjoyed that he would not lose a year. Although I thought about the fact that he would be away from us, I didn't quite realize it. Because I didn't want to think about his absence, *how could I bear this conscious separation?*

We started to look for a small apartment near the university for my brother through the Internet. It was difficult to find an apartment, even more difficult to find an apartment in a big city, especially in certain parts of the city. Rents were also very high, even though the square footage of the apartments was small. What happened to you, you had to endure. There was nothing you could do about it.

During those first six months, I couldn't get out of the stress of exams, either at work or at home. Things even happened that I had not expected. Don't just call this profession hairdressing, it was like getting my PhD. What did we hairdressers have to do with anatomy? Only because we performed cosmetic skin care. Well, it was a satisfying profession.

My boss had helped me a lot but my other colleagues were not very interested. Since I was the first employee who had attended the master school, the others became cold and stayed away from me. My boss said, "I'd rather you work with your models in the salon, then you can take care of your theory in peace." She was cordial and helpful.

However, it was my private decision to attend the master school, it had nothing to do with my job. After all, I really wanted to do it for myself. If you can take a step forward in education and development, it was a good thing. Don't stop people who want to do that ... Laziness is not a good habit. My boss used to say to me, - even though she didn't have to do it:

"You're going to stay away from the customers for a while, leave the other work and start studying on your models for the exams."

She emphasized this pattern again and again and that gave me a lot of strength. "We will still achieve many successes together, we will have many projects together," she said, cheering me up with such words.

In this intense and difficult phase, I received a lot of support from my family. I was no longer afraid of the written exam as in the first days but experienced an exciting situation.

Suat, too, had devoted himself to testing. As I had predicted, not even a click was heard in the house. We would all get through this time. Finally, I had passed the written exam and three weeks later I was to present my craft skills individually. I had worked hard on that.

First Suat had received the news that he had passed, even before me. After two weeks had passed, I also received the news.

Yes, I had successfully obtained my master craftsman's certificate, a great burden had fallen from me. When the certificates and diplomas were distributed, I was called to the podium like the other future master graduates. They presented me with a bouquet of flowers, a certificate of achievement and recognition, my credentials and my certificate of passing the exam. I was very happy, it was a very nice feeling. It was a very difficult phase but thank God I had overcome it.

My boss had my employment contract changed and wanted to officially hire me as a master. My salary was to be increased. The salary of a hairdresser with a master title was not as high as others thought. My other colleagues were not happy about this at all, it was obvious in every way and they let me feel it.

My boss told me that one work day she had planned a meeting with all of us over dinner or breakfast.

"Everyone is to write the day that suits them on a piece of paper and turn it in to my office," she asked everyone. We had all done exactly what she had asked. For the next Wednesday evening after work, she reserved a table for us at a Greek restaurant. Suddenly, our boss left the hair salon and in a hurry. It was obvious that she first had to take care of other things than the meeting.

In the evening, my boss called my cell phone. I took the call and was amazed.

"Hello Yasemin, where are you?" she inquired. I quickly explained that I had been shopping and was not home yet, whereupon she told me that she would be with me in an hour. She had something to discuss with me, she was already on her way. "*I hope it's something good.* Of course you are welcome, I will be home," I answered her before ending the conversation.

When I came home after shopping, I had immediately informed the others at home that my boss was coming. Our house was clean as always, thank God, we were not stressed.

The doorbell rang, my boss was there. She was in a hurry. Immediately I received her in the living room. Since she liked Turkish tea, I had already made tea before she arrived. Everything was ready, I had taken out my porcelain service and arranged it on the tray. After serving the tea, I said, "Here, I'm listening, what happened?" She had kept me guessing.

"My mother had a very serious stroke, she is in the hospital. I can take over my mother's hair salon for a week or two, that's not a problem. But what will happen to the salon after that? She has a lot of customers, I spent my childhood in that salon, I can't bear to close it or hand it over. I can't bring myself to do that. I can say that it is like a family heirloom, it means a lot to me.

My mother's condition is very critical, I don't know when she will recover! I immediately thought of you. You've finished your master's degree. Would you work in my mother's salon for a while? Since you are also doing other tasks in the salon, I will pay you too, I have no doubt about that. As it was agreed with my mother, we will continue the rental thing like this. I am not in favor of changing anything in your contract," she submitted to me.

In other words, the entire responsibility for the hair salon on the first floor of our house would be mine, with everything that went with it. In fact, this was a very good step for me and a very good opportunity. I wanted to educate myself in a different way and gain new experience and I wanted to enjoy this responsibility.

Since my employer would remain the same, I didn't hesitate for long and gladly accepted her offer. Besides, it was only one flight of stairs away from my house. What could be better than this! "No problem, I gladly accept such a nice offer," I replied.

Finally, I expressed my get-well wishes and my sorrow for her mother. Then I explained how important it was to stick together in difficult times.

"I thank you, Yasemin, for not leaving me alone in these difficult days. At our meeting, I will also invite the employees of my mother's hair salon. We will continue our meeting as a big team. I will also inform the other employees about this change in a speech that day. I will explain that from the day you start, the responsibility of the salon and the staff will be yours and on the days I am not available, the responsibility of my own salon will also be yours. It will be better if you learn it from me first," she explained.

Then the time flew by. On the day of the meeting, my boss mentioned some of the changes that would take place. Some people were not at all happy with these changes and the position of master assigned to me. There were also some who seemed to be against it. These were people who had nothing to do with the craft and just had a personal problem with me.

My boss wondered about these holdouts. "I didn't ask for your opinion, I just stated my decision and the changes that will take place from now on. It's up to you whether you accept it or not. As long as you work in my salon, you must accept it. Otherwise, give me a written statement that you want to leave your job. As you have heard, my mother had a stroke and is in the hospital. I need those who support me these days and I don't have the strength to deal with those who don't," she spoke harshly.

In other words, either you accept or you don't! If not, that's your problem, she said briefly and politely.

The employees of her mother's salon were pleased with this decision. There were no problems with them. The problem was those who were jealous of me and couldn't stand me. My boss had already given them the answer. After the announcement of the new decisions, I began to work as a master in her mother's salon. From now on, my work system would be completely different. She told me that in the first days she would come more often to the hair salon and that she would show me other subjects like accounting, income and expenses. It was not long before I had completely taken over the responsibility.

Since I had previously worked one day a week in her mother's salon, I knew the work system of this salon and began my new job without difficulty. After about two weeks came the news of the death of her mother. Although she was happy to have organized this change in advance, my boss went through a very difficult time.

My boss had also not unnamed her mother's hair salon. The house where we lived was now her inheritance. She had not changed any of our previous arrangements with her mother. Things went on exactly as before. I was in charge of my work and my duties and my master's certificate now hung on the wall in the entryway of the hair salon. My prizes from all the competitions were also displayed at the entrance to the salon.

If you remember, we were looking for an apartment for Suat. He had started his studies but we hadn't found a suitable apartment yet. He said he could live in a dorm until he found one. Both Suat and I did not want that. Three to seven students used one room. Shower stalls and toilets were shared. It was not a nice atmosphere. After about two months, we found a small apartment that was suitable and close to the university.

Since Suat liked it, the contract was signed and my brother lived there since then, since he studied in Stuttgart. He had to study for a total of eight semesters, which was a total of four years. Whenever it was possible, he came home on holidays and weekends.

After her last year of high school, Kiraz, just like her brother, went to a preparatory school for university. This phase was very important for her future. We emphasized this very carefully.

Was there anything better than learning and educating yourself? I don't understand at all the people who were in the way and wanted to be in the way. Those who want to learn should do so. Instead of being an ignorant and uneducated society, it was better to be useful to the country and society. It was necessary. One had to learn, develop and educate first!

We had continued to spend our vacations in Türkiye on a regular basis. In this respect, our everyday life had not changed. As far as possible, I kept my two siblings away from the stress of everyday life, preferring that they focus only on their schooling.

In the meantime, I had gotten a lien on my aunt's house through my lawyer. I didn't let any of them off the hook. Even in the midst of my work and my daily hustle and bustle, there was no way I was going to put these matters off until tomorrow.

Their house was auctioned off so they lost their house at a very low price. If the rights of orphans are exploited, won't God let them get away with it? So I had taken their house, including furniture, their equipment and their cars.

Seventy-five thousand euros was all I could squeeze out. The rest was paid in monthly installments. Every month they transferred the installments to the account of my lawyer, whom I had immediately set upon them so that I could use the money to pay for my master school.

Then I had bought myself a small car because I desperately needed a car for my work. Sometimes I also went shopping, instead of ordering, I bought the hairdressing material myself. At that time my boss gave me her car. We somehow managed but it was not a permanent solution. It was better that way, I was very glad that I had my driver's license at that time.

In order for Suat to get along better, I had bought a small kitchen and had it installed in his apartment. Together with my brother, we shared the rent of Suat's new home. We also wanted to contribute to the costs of Kiraz's university education. Suat had secretly started working on the side so that he would not be too much of a burden on me. At one point, he refused to accept the money I sent him and returned it to my account.

When I called him and asked why the money was put back into my account, he explained, "I'm working, I found a job, you're getting too burdened with the rent and other expenses. Thank God, I can work, I want to take care of the expenses other than rent from now on myself." The decision was made by my brother, he was the one who knew best but I insisted that he should not do it. But in vain ... It was useless ... He was obsessed with it ... For a few months I would not be able to get this idea out of his head anyway, so I let him.

Today, exactly three weeks later, my maternal aunt was released from prison. Four years and six months had passed. The time flew by. We still kept our address a secret. None of the letters my lawyer had sent to her contained our address or any information about us. I had insisted on this for our own safety.

In the meantime, I had filed another criminal complaint against my paternal aunt's husband after she had moved in with us. After this criminal complaint, three more years and five months were added to his sentence. So my brother-in-law was to spend many years in prison. That was very reassuring and good news.

How could he sexually abuse me and not be punished?

No one could lay a hand on me against my will. They shouldn't... I think the law should be tougher in this matter.

If they needed treatment, let them be treated. Nobody objected because if they had a healthy soul, would such people ever commit such terrible crimes? I don't think so, I was for their punishment. My brother-in-law was punished for the abuse he had inflicted on me and I was glad of it.

My aunt was still living with us today. So we all lived under the same roof.

A strong woman is like a good future!

CHAPTER
29

My boss and I still participated in competitions. From that time I had won cups, up to world championships. That gave me more confidence and security in my work. I had benefited greatly from these competitions. We had participated in fairs as a salon team and had performed on stage. So my boss, who liked to educate herself further and would like to educate herself further ...

Exactly one week ago, my boss called me on my cell phone at the end of the work day. She wanted to see me again urgently, so she asked when I would be free. Two days later, we both closed the salons in the evening and met at a nearby Italian restaurant. While we were having a drink, she immediately got down to business and told me that she wanted to give up the salon, that she would sell the house to me if I agreed and that it was too exhausting and costly for her. "One salon is enough for me, the other one frankly made me a little tired," she confessed.

Without taking her eyes off me, she asked, "Yes, Yasemin, what do you say? This is a good opportunity for you too! The salon is nice and runs well, you have employees who do their work properly and do not cause any problems. Think about it calmly and let me know your decision by the end of the week."

That was a good idea and a really great offer. Of course, I didn't give an answer that day. "I'll let you know my decision after I think about it," I replied. My boss came prepared, of course. She had brought everything she had for the house and the salon in terms of documents. So she had handed me three folders so that all my questions could be answered.

"You know, I lost my husband before my mother. If my husband had lived, I would have been able to cope. But in this situation, I'm alone. I have my own house. After the death of my mother and husband, I am definitely not able to carry a second salon and the house where you live. The most suitable and appropriate for me is you and your family. I would not offer it to anyone else. I would go on like this until I couldn't do it anymore. But a trustworthy person, like you are, who has already been present in my business and personal life for years, I trust. I know who you are. There is no doubt about it. You are best suited for me, I want you to know that," she confessed to me.

In fact, the sale price of the house in its current state exceeded two hundred and thirty-seven thousand euros. Of course, if the hair salon equipment is added, this figure increases a little. The total price was currently two hundred and ninety-five thousand euros. "But I have no intention of taking this money from you. From the first day you started your job with me until now, you have never let me down but supported me in every way.

My grandparents bought this house, they were the first to run a hair salon. Then they gave the salon to my mother and my grandmother and grandfather continued to live on the upper floor of the house. First my grandmother died, then my grandfather died shortly after. My mother had her own house. She lived in her own house for many years. She didn't take care of a tenant or make repairs. When I realized it wasn't working, I had the house renovated. It became habitable, then you moved in. From the entrance to the house to the garden, everywhere you and your family worked. You take good and careful care of the house. I don't need this house but you need it. That's why I want to take a big step with you, I'm not waiting for your answer now. Think carefully and give me your answer by the end of this week.

I'm only asking you for ninety thousand euros!" she suggested.

The ninety thousand euros she asked for was nothing. It was really official, nothing. The next morning, before I went to work, I immediately discussed the matter with my lawyer. My boss had given me the records of the house in case I wanted to investigate something. My attorney told me to e-mail the records immediately, which I did.

"If you can, Yasemin, don't let this opportunity pass you by. Even if it were auctioned off, this house in such a condition would not sell for ninety thousand euros. The price would drop to at least two hundred and ten thousand euros if it were auctioned. Let's say it is two hundred thousand euros and you can assume that you have profited from this deal with ninety thousand euros. Don't wait, take it. This is a once-in-a-lifetime opportunity, Yasemin, don't miss it, if you have any sense, grab it right now," he advised me.

In the evening after work, I had talked about it with my siblings and my aunt. Just like my lawyer, they kept saying, "This is a once-in-a-lifetime opportunity." Although I had never thought of anything like this, it was the only topic I could think of. So I had talked to my brother because his opinion was important to me, too.

Without thinking twice, he said, "Buy the house!" They had all agreed. It was up to me. Through my aunt's fine, I received a total of seventy-five thousand euros. Through my siblings' school and education expenses, the last remaining instalments of the master school and my brother's household goods - I was left with sixty-five thousand euros. Although my brother offered, "I will make up the rest," I had not accepted it.

So I called my bank and made an appointment during my lunch break. I went prepared, the bank employee was also prepared for our appointment because I had already told him on the phone that it was about a loan. As soon as I arrived, we started the process. I needed exactly twenty-five thousand euros to raise the money for the house. I had applied to the bank for a loan of fifty- thousand euros. After my loan was approved, the procedure to transfer the house into my name was initiated.

Now I was the owner of a house and a workplace.

Sometimes things have not to go well before they get better.

Yasemin's Struggle

CHAPTER
30

Lately, I have not had a free minute. I was in an extraordinary hurry. The way I was going was very busy. In the evenings after work, I also did the accounting work at home. It was unpredictable whether I would be able to take responsibility for the decisions made or not. Whenever possible, I tried to do these tasks at times between working at the salon so that my work did not extend to my personal time. Very quickly I managed to do what was related to work during working hours.

I still had to deal with my former boss. Sometimes, when I traveled to Türkiye, she even came with me. Both privately and at work, we socialized with each other. She also came when I was traveling alone to see the salon I was running and I went to her salon. After a while, I found myself in a relationship of togetherness. We had gotten along very well. Everything had developed spontaneously in this way.

I had been running my hair salon for about a year. But I had never thought of changing the name of the salon. We had now developed a routine. Kiraz, on the other hand, was still studying her preparatory years at university. She had one more year until graduation. Suat had one and a half years left to finish his degree. At first I said it was four years, now it was only one and a half years. During the vacations, Suat worked at my brother's holding company. He had started to lay the foundation for his pre-studies and had a good position in our holding company and a job before the end of his studies.

However, Kiraz was rather undecided about what she wanted to become or what she wanted to study. She vacillated back and forth between two options because she actually wanted to do both very much. On the one hand, she wanted to become a sworn translator in her native language but on the other hand, she also wanted to study English. She also spoke German without an accent. In addition, she wanted to further her education in foreign languages. She could speak English like an Englishman. I was proud of both of them. Both had grown up in my hands, in my arms with the affection of a mother but I did not have the right to take away important decisions about their future. *How could I hinder them both when I was concerned for their welfare?*

So from yesterday to today, a lot of time had passed.

Whereas before I had struggled in life, now I had overcome my struggle and was living a life full of peace, with people I loved and trusted. I was experiencing very beautiful developments and moving forward with my steps. Although my wounds bled from time to time and hurt again, I did not want to return to the old years. I would not let that happen again because

I was stronger now, I was not the old Yasemin anymore. No one would hurt me anymore. No one would bend my upright posture, I was determined to do that. Even if it hurt, I would not let it happen, I would protect myself stronger without becoming a victim again. Accidents, you could not see out, that was something else.

May God protect each of us - all of us - from these days (Ameen).

I learned that my former boss had breast cancer. I was very sad about that, I didn't want to leave her alone. She underwent surgery and one of her breasts was removed. A little later, after she had undergone chemotherapy, her beautiful hair had gradually fallen out. This illness had exhausted her. Except for one or two relatives, there was no one left in her family. It was not enough but she did not even have a brother or sister. While she was struggling with this disease all alone, she had another surgery and her second breast was also removed. She had lost a lot of weight, she did not accept herself in this condition. The responsibility for the two salons was given to me. She had a power of attorney issued and signed so that I could make all decisions regarding her salon. That's how much she had trusted me.

Without realizing it, we had formed a small but powerful team. She also had a son. We met one day after work. His mother's condition was very serious at that time. I wanted to talk to him personally in more depth about these issues.

His mother had always wanted him to attend a master school and earn a master's certificate. No one could surpass her in terms of self-improvement and education. She had also maintained this behavior, telling her son over and over again, "Come on, son, you will need it in the future, do it, do it, do it." This is not a lie, this is a fact! He was never interested. Nor did he feel the need to enroll in a master school.

After the coffee was served, as God was my witness, I told him what I thought of him. We were engrossed in conversation. He was a person who respected me very much. Although he was my employer's son at the time, to this day he had no objections when I had the last word in the salon. Moreover, he was not the one who brought it to the point because I brought it to the table. In this way, the communication was mutual.

Suddenly he took a deep breath and propped his elbows on the table, then said, "Okay, I'll enroll in the master school." That was all, he said nothing else and I had never asked him for anything else.

Again I experienced a turning point, again I felt that something would change in my life. My former boss had stopped fighting because she did not accept herself in that condition. She was in very bad shape. When I visited her in the hospital one evening, I told her that her son wanted to enroll in the master school, had filled out the enrollment papers and sent them off. "This is good news, I'm very happy about it," she whispered weakly. Then she handed me an envelope. "Please open it at home and look at it in peace," she asked me weakly.

She sat up slightly.

"Yasemin, I have something to discuss with you. Please, listen to me first! Look how far we have come, Yasemin. Where we were yesterday and where we are today. I said when I first saw you that this girl had something, and I was right. Yasemin, it is a great wealth for me to know you. I learned a lot from you, even if I didn't say it. I have a good knowledge of human nature. You are very hardworking, determined and ambitious. When you have a goal, you don't let it out of your sight.

You strive until you reach your goal. I admire you and am glad I had the opportunity to meet you. You are a friend to have by your side on a bad day. You have made a place for yourself in the hearts of our family, you have endeared yourself. You are one of us, you know that. In that short time, you became one of my closest friends. We shared our work, our business, trusted each other and had each other's back.

My hairdressing salon is very busy, I always attach importance to comfort. Unfortunately, I can't trust my son in this regard. My son has been trying to get me to do this for years. In short, he has made me tired. He has made me work unnecessarily. I don't trust my hair salon to anyone but you. I have been very good to you. The furniture in my salon costs no less than one hundred and eighty thousand euros, it is a shiny, wooden and high-quality salon. You yourself worked for me for a while. One hundred and twenty-five thousand euros can be calculated on average for the materials. Special high-gloss tiles, you know that better than I do, Yasemin. You know very well about my customers, income and expenses.

But I don't have all that in mind because I have enjoyed my life to the fullest and have kept both my son and my mother alive to the best of my ability. I have always had a beautiful and rich life, never lived in poverty.

The only thing I ask is because when I die, my son will be orphaned. Be a family to him. We all get along fine. I have talked to my son, he knows I will talk to you about these issues. You know we don't pay rent for the store because we own it. For the inside of the store I want ten thousand euros from you. I'm handing it over to you as it is. You can see that from the notarization in the envelope.

I am not a Muslim but I believe that Allah is one and the same. Injustices done to people should not be returned by the same people. Maybe Allah made it possible for me to return these things to you because you deserved them. Weren't you the one who said that nothing happens by chance or without reason?

My son didn't object to my decision, he didn't even talk about it. After all, I am the one who makes the decision and he respected my decision. I'm not asking you for ten thousand euros up front.

Please don't leave my son alone during master school and don't leave him alone after school. Create a family between you. Please don't leave him alone!" she begged me.

After these last words, my former employer began to cry softly, sighing sadly and withdrawn. She was not crying because of her illness but because of the fact that her son would be left alone. Of course, I was also very sad. Events were overflowing that it was hard to believe.

But I did not have the opportunity to make a decision because such a dialogue had taken place between us. It was as if decisions had been made. She was sitting on the bed looking old. She had hidden her face from me because she had been crying.

While listening to her, I sat on the chair at the foot of the bed and held her hand with one hand. Thoughtfully, I stood up, opened my arms and hugged her tightly. My throat was tight. I was faced with novelties I had never expected. "I have no more worries and can close my eyes forever and ever," she breathed emotionally. I was moved by this.

Even though I kept telling myself, *"Be strong, stay strong, you have to be strong,"* it was in vain. It was too late. My tears began to flow in streams. It had been a long time since I had cried. In the atmosphere at that moment, I didn't have the strength to suppress my feelings. But I didn't want to, to be honest. We were not machines, we were human beings after all. We have to include our feelings from time to time.

The hospital's visiting hours were over, it was already closed. We were so engrossed that I had to hurriedly pack up and leave that evening. After that last visit, I was not quite myself. God knows in what condition I came home.

As soon as I entered the house, my aunt asked, "What's wrong, dear? What's the matter with you? What happened to my beautiful one?" When I heard this question, my chin began to tremble slightly. I could not shake off the feelings from the hospital. The name of my former employer was Claudia.

Day by day, she faded before my eyes. So I talked to my aunt, we went to the kitchen and sat down at the table. My aunt listened to me quietly, without interrupting me.

After we finished talking, I called my brother. The decisions had already been made, Claudia had transferred the salon into my name. It was notarized in the envelope. I was not happy that the hair salon was in my name, Claudia's condition and her situation outweighed my feelings.

Then I called her son Tobias and asked him to come over if he had time. He came over in the evening in less than half an hour. So I told him about my conversation with his mother at the hospital. "I have this information," he said, sipping his coffee. "When you get your master's certificate, I'll turn your salon over to you, and you can run it," I offered.

"Absolutely not, no!" was his hard and determined answer. "And why not?", I inquired. To which he replied, "Don't any of you listen to me? I don't want to do this job, I don't want to do this job, I don't want to do this job. The family profession was instilled in all of us by my grandmother's mother and continued for years. While I have been struggling for years to break this chain, you still want to tie me to the hair salon. Today you enrolled me in the master school. I'm enrolled, I don't know where this is going!"

While Tobias was talking like this, I heard for the first time that the child had been forced into this profession. I didn't know it was like that. As we expanded our conversation with questions like, "What do you want to do?" we came to different decisions together and were able to end our conversation that night on a positive note. That day, I was so exhausted that I didn't know what time I had gone to bed that evening.

Three weeks later came the news of Claudia's death. She had recently stopped fighting. We had all been through a lot at that time.

Although Tobias said he wanted to drop out of master school, he did not. I thought *that our conversation had worked,* that he had digested what he had said and thought about it again. These were good developments.

Due to the fact that everything had developed spontaneously, I owned two hair salons. I was thrown into a very big responsibility. Both salons were not far from each other. In this respect, luck was on my side. The first year was very busy and exhausting. I accept that but with God's will I had managed to overcome it in time.

My brother Suat was now counting his days at the university. He was getting closer to the end day by day. Now he was too busy with his exams. His last year was a disastrous year. He was constantly studying for his exams under very intense conditions. Meanwhile, Kiraz had completed her university preparatory years. Everything was happening so fast. In the meantime, a year had passed since Claudia died and I was shuttling back and forth between the two salons.

Sometimes you did nothing but everything happened by itself. Sometimes you tried and tried but you wasted your energy in vain. It was all fate and luck, I believe.

Tobias had successfully completed master school. Now he held his master craftsman's certificate in his hand. "I'm glad I didn't drop out," he later confessed but he didn't want to work in the hair salon anymore, he had left the team. Later, he started working at the Wella company, which manufactured hairdressing supplies. His work was also good and he warmed up with his work. Now I gave him all my orders for hairdressing supplies and again we found common ground in the business environment. Then he started a relationship with a young, smart and beautiful girl.

When he saw our life in Türkiye, he said, "Are you stupid, why don't you go back to Türkiye? You have such a nice life, why don't you live there?" Nihat and Tobias got to know each other right away. When they went to Holding together a few times, my brother offered him a job. He also told his girlfriend that his job was ready for interviews abroad. Tobias and his girlfriend (Stefanie / nicknamed Steffi) kept to themselves for a while and after half an hour they said they had accepted my brother's offer. It was incredible, I was very happy about this news. From where to where ... Wherever one was destined. Tobias had not left us and we had not left Tobias.

Both lived with my brother until they got their own house in order. Tobias, a man of some standing, refused all offers of financial support from my brother and with his own savings they settled in their own house. Each of them was now responsible for his own affairs.

Then when Suat graduated, he followed them because he wanted to continue his life in Türkiye. While my brother was preparing for another business field, my brother said to Suat: "No, you will be with me. From now on, both of us, two brothers, will run this business," he said, putting his hand on Suat's shoulder. To be honest, I didn't expect it to happen like this either.

Then, when the two of them were alone in the office, my brother said to Suat, "Before our father died, he had instructed everyone in charge at the holding company to show me everything so that I could learn everything as quickly as possible and this phase was very useful for me. Since I found it useful and beneficial, I want you to go through the same phase because we will be at the same level."

My brother Suat felt very honored when my brother spoke like that. He never thought that everything would turn out like this. As I said before, everyone gets what is due to them.

Once again, I had reached the end of my cassette. Now I would take a break from my recordings for a while. Consciously, I left myself to busy days. I had hired two young people who had started their professional training. I would devote myself to them, to my work and to my family. Goodbye.

If someone is helping you in a difficult situation,
even if you need help,
it is not out of desire to help, but in my love.

Yasemin's Struggle

CHAPTER
31

Incredibly, I had reached the end of my story. The years flew by. In the meantime I had become thirty-one years old. And what kind of Yasemin had life made of me from then until now? I could not pack what I had experienced into three thick books.

"Today after all this time I feel the need to speak again. People forget themselves in their daily busyness and routine, in the hustle and bustle. I led a monotonous life but it was very colorful. Since I loved my work and my family very much, their presence brought color into my life, even if it was monotonous. Today I was a little melancholy. I was alone at home, it was Sunday! Kiraz started her studies, she was luckier than Suat, her apartment was right next to the university. Now we were to go through the same thing with Kiraz. During Suat's study time we had had our first experiences with him. So I could approach Kiraz with a little more awareness, maturity and experience.

My aunt was in the hospital. The burn marks on her skin were treated with light therapy. She had to stay in the hospital until Wednesday but she benefited from this light treatment. It was necessary. At least eight times a year she had to undergo this inpatient treatment in the hospital.

I felt like melancholy today, I want to spend a very quiet, calm and relaxed day. So I put my feet up on the couch, leaned back against the cushions, threw a blanket over me and took my dictaphone in my hand, after all this time again.

My small wooden chest, where I kept all my private things, stood on the table with the lid open. Over a cup of coffee, I began to thoroughly analyze my inner self once again. Of course, the old times came to my mind. All the things that had happened lined up one after another before my eyes. I had disappeared into the distance. Hey, the world of lies, from where to where In the depths, the lying world. That made me what I am today.

For about a year and a half I had undergone treatment to get rid of my internal wounds and I was glad that I had done so. In the end, I didn't regret it at all and I recommend it to all of you. I was able to deal more consciously with my pain and the negativities I had experienced and I was able to live more consciously with those feelings. Being able to look at events from a different perspective had changed my perspective on many issues.

Who was I dealing with and who was I fighting? What was right? What was wrong? I had processed and digested them all one by one and I had a different inner peace. It was a feeling I had never experienced before.

I had expanded my hair salon to a third. How? Let me tell you ...

This situation, like the others, had developed spontaneously. One day, when I was working, two women and a man entered the salon. Thank God, both of my salons were very busy and located in the center. Therefore, there was not much time for small talk, or rather, there was no time at all. I had made an appointment for those who came so that we could talk in peace.

On the day of our appointment, they arrived on time. Immediately we retreated to my office in the back of the salon to talk in peace. There they revealed to me that they didn't really think much of their employer and that at this rate they were going to lose their jobs. They were in a state of closure. The good thing was that the hair salon was in the center, like my other two salons, even with one of them on the same street.

After I finished talking to all three of them, I asked the question, "What do you expect from me?" Their answer was that they wanted me to take over the salon. After our meeting was over, we said goodbye. I had been very confused by this situation. A week or two later, I happened to meet the owner of the salon on my morning commute to work. There was no such thing as coincidence, let's call it fate, kismet in other words.

We greeted each other and I asked him on what day he would be available to talk: "I am always available, we can talk now," he offered.

However, I figured that *a person who is responsible for his job can not always be available.* So we had arranged a day and talked, then we had agreed and I had taken over the hair salon. A little innovation was needed in the interiors. The workforce had remained the same, plus I had hired two young people for vocational training. A master craftswoman was also at the beginning of her new duties. Thus my third hairdressing salon had been added. Everything comes from God ... Even if it was difficult and exhausting, I would make it as long as my health and well-being allowed. Those who know it, know how difficult it is. I had worked very hard for it.

Suat always came to us in Germany, not on vacations but on extended weekends. Either he stayed with us from Thursday to Friday or Sunday, or from Saturday to Monday and Tuesday. He had also worked hard. We were aware of the daily hustle and bustle and our responsibility.

Eight years had passed. As far as I had researched, Nurgül had moved and I did not know her new address, she had changed the city. I wouldn't have knocked on her door spontaneously anyway unless it was an emergency, that would be different.

But the privilege of going to her home was over for me. So I had searched for her on the internet but I had not found her address or phone number on the internet. Then through social media I had found her, at first she had not believed it was me. Only after we had talked on the phone via video call. Although she had no contact with me, despite my sudden and unannounced departure, she had still protected me.

"I'm on my way to Frankfurt," I told her and asked her if she had time for a spontaneous meeting. When she answered in the affirmative, I jumped into the car and drove to her place. Since I really didn't have much time, we had only spent fifteen or twenty minutes together.

What had been going through my mind the whole way there was, *what if she called me all kinds of things?* I guessed I couldn't disagree with her because she was right. If such a situation were to occur, I had come to the conclusion that everything she said would be right and justified. After all, I had disappeared for eight years, then I faced her as if nothing had happened. *Was that possible?* Of course, if there was something to say on this subject, *I would have kept silent out of respect and love.*

As far as I had heard, Nurgül had published her first "ANA" book. There were authorgram days and book launch days. In a way, she would savor her first experiences with the ANA book.

She would savor her experience of her first ANA feelings in the book world.

I also saw that she shared from time to time that her book "Yasemin's Despair" was in progress. Nurgül had not given up hope on me yet. She was still writing to Yasemins. May her hands never suffer! I admitted that I had been ungrateful to her by hiding and disappearing from the market for eight years. When I had first turned to my aunt Meral, I should have turned to Nurgül as well. There is no cure, for the dead, there is a saying. Of course, I admitted my mistake.

Nurgül approached me sincerely and warmly in her old habit. She was the person I trusted. Although we had not seen each other for eight years, she would not give up her good behavior. She had never approached me in such a way that I had to account for those eight years. When I told her about my situation, she said, "You must have known something." Without any insult or resentment. Without being asked, we were able to face each other years later, exactly one and a half years ago.

Another year and a half had passed. Was it just me, or did time really pass so quickly?

When we said goodbye, I had handed her a voice recording assistant, which contained a cassette. She had just stared silently as I handed it to her and then we parted ways again. From that day until today, I had had no contact with Nurgül and had not spoken to her on the phone. Furthermore, I had only sent her the cassettes I had recorded by mail. On the condition that I kept my address secret. If I said that time is gold, then from now on Nurgül was one of the people I would not want to cut out of my life. If it is our fate, God will bring us together again.

Today I had finally written to her on social media to tell her I wanted to meet in person, but this time I was hoping to keep in permanent contact with here. But she had not seen or read my message yet.

For the last year or two, I had been talking about my daily life. We had shared our trump cards with those who had wronged me and persecuted me. Each of them had been punished according to law and justice but there was also life after death. May God forgive and give guidance.

Let's move on to the state of the perpetrators after the injustice committed. Although so many years had passed, some of them were still being punished for their deeds and in a big way. Their families were broken up, their homes destroyed, they were still in prison. *So what more could I say?* I said divine justice from now on.

Your heart, which has returned to the place of fire, will be heavy in revenge, humanity cannot bear!

Yasemin's Struggle

CHAPTER
32

As I spoke, I found peace and all the knots were gradually untied. With God's permission, I was put on the right path. I had started praying two and a half years ago. God knows I had difficulties in the early days but I had overcome that phase. I prayed in my heart and thanked God for granting me these holy feelings. It was a different peace of mind, a clean, holy, untouchable feeling. Thanks be to God Almighty.

It didn't take long for Kiraz's university education to end. "Let's all go back to Türkiye together," she said during our phone calls.

I had thought about this a lot. One day, when Kiraz came home one weekend, my aunt, Kiraz and I discussed this matter calmly and at length. The decision was made. Yes, I had decided to return to our homeland forever and we were able to convince my aunt as well.

While I was still considering whether the treatment for her burns would be better in Germany, my brother Nihat said to me on the phone, "Put that idea out of your mind right now. There are so many excellent professors, doctors and physicians in Türkiye, so don't worry your head about it."

My aunt then replied, "I'm with you, I'm in." So the decision was made. We were going to return to Türkiye forever, to our homeland. Until then, I had to sell the three hair salons and the house I managed and owned. It looked like I was going to have busy days again.

A buyer was immediately found for the salon that Claudia had left to me. "What if the building of the salon also wants to be bought?", I asked Tobias.

"I think I would sell it then, not rent it," he said.

So I had handed over the salon to the Wella company, Tobias had come to Germany for a short time for the sale.

At dinner, I handed Tobias the entire sale of the salon which I had left to him. He looked at me stunned. "That's your right, you have established a new responsibility in Türkiye. You need the money. Don't resist it," I told him and we embraced in brotherly affection. Yes, I had such a memory of Tobias.

As for the hair salon under my house, I had talked to my master. If he agreed, I tell him that I planned to give him the salon until our return to Türkiye. So I was going to sell him the house and the hair salon, he was still young, had been married for a few months and had settled down. When I received the commitment from him, I was very relieved. My salons were well running, worked well and were centrally located.

Kiraz was preparing for the exam, our days were getting shorter and shorter. Four siblings intend to visit the Umrah. May God grant us to see and visit these holy lands. My brother had registered all of us to visit the Umrah (pilgrimage to Mecca) because I really wanted my uncle Osman, aunt Meral, the driver Ahmet and my aunt to come. I talked to my brother, "Yes, I'll sign them all up," he offered.

Aunt Meral was touched and cried with joy. I could not spare her.

While I was recording the cassette, I received a reply from Nurgül to the message I had sent her about a week ago. This time I did not write mysteriously but she would recognize me immediately from my message. So we agreed on a day to meet. I think it was safe to say that I was already looking forward to the day we would meet. My last message was that I would call, after which I deleted the account I had opened on social media. So with that attitude, I had let Nurgül near me again without giving my contact information. This time, when I called, I would call without keeping my number a secret. There were no more situations where I was followed. The danger had disappeared.

Towards evening I called her. When she told me she was in the hospital and couldn't talk for long, I was quite worried.

She had had a serious operation and it was clear from her voice. When I learned which hospital she was in, I set out the next morning without wasting any time. That same evening I had decided that I could not yet give her my last cassette. It was October 2015 and I visited Nurgül the next morning. The drive took exactly six hours, I set off at around five in the morning. At the hospital, I knocked on the door of her room Slowly I opened the door and entered. Nurgül was lying semi-conscious on her hospital bed. She was hooked up to a lot of apparatus and was on a drip. I was devastated to find her in this state and I did not yet know what was going on.

Apparently she had heard my footsteps because she turned her head toward the door, away from the wall. As soon as she recognized me, she called out weakly, "Yasemin!" So I stepped closer to her bed. "Nurgül," I began to speak, stroking her head, her hair and her face. She had been operated on three days ago and still couldn't stand up. It was also difficult for her to speak. I had no intention of tiring her with my visit. I looked at her and after a few sentences she fainted again. This must have been the result of the operation. So I pulled the chair to the edge of her bed and held her hand for about an hour or two. She was still asleep ...

In between, I put on my jacket, went to the hospital cafeteria, bought a hot cocoa and sat down next to her again. On the

Internet, I booked a room in the nearest hotel for three days because I didn't want to leave Nurgül alone.

When I returned to her room at noon, Nurgül was praying, although she could not turn to the left or right on her sickbed. I waited in silence for the end. When she finished, she called out to me once again, weakened, "Yasemin!" With my back pressed against the window, I now approached her bed. "Here I am!", I answered.

"You have come, welcome, my little rose," she greeted me warmly again. I quickly pulled the chair back to her bedside and held her hand.

"I think we've come to the end of your revenge, haven't we, Yasemin?" she asked me. "Yes, we are at the end, thank God," I confirmed.

"I edited all the cassettes you sent. My book entitled Yasemin's Struggle would be in my hands right now, but since the first edition was a terrible edition, it became a complaint. Even though I had worked so meticulously on it, such a mishap happened to me. But don't worry, I have a contract with a new publisher and it will be printed again. 2015 was a very bad year for me. As soon as I enter 2016, I will start a new page as if I were starting all over again. The book will be published by that date, Yasemin," she had told me.

"Stop thinking about the book, how are you? What happened? Why did you have surgery? What's wrong with you? Tell me about you," I demanded angrily. "I'm fine, I'm over it now, thank God," she said.

I wanted to know what was going on, what was wrong with her? But I didn't press her too hard because she was physically weak and I didn't want to press her with my questions. Sometimes she would fall asleep again in her hospital bed. So I went back down to the hospital cafeteria, from where I called the hair salon and told the master that he would have to manage on his own until I returned. Finally, I was confronted with a situation that I had not expected.

When I returned to her room around six o'clock in the evening, the nurses accompanied by the doctor tried to mobilize Nurgül. Then, when the nurse saw me at the door, she closed the door from the inside. Therefore, I waited outside the door and heard her being forced to move from inside. The fact that her voices occasionally came through to me distorted with pain overwhelmed me with a flood of emotion. When I could no longer hold back my tears, I realized that I could not face her in this state. After making myself presentable in the visitors' restroom on the second floor of the hospital, I continued to wait outside her door. It was not long before three nurses and four doctors came out of her room.

"You can come in now," they said as they left. I immediately entered Nurgül's room. When she saw me, she gave me a slight smile and turned her head a little to the side.

At that moment, a feeling of guilt arose in my heart. The way she smiled at me in that state made me feel guilty toward her. I knew I had made a mistake by not telling Nurgül my whereabouts, my residence and my contact information. "Are you okay?" she asked weakly. "Don't be unnecessarily unfair to yourself, Yasemin, my dear. Don't carry such feelings in your heart unnecessarily," she answered me. "Everyone lives their own destiny, we do too," she replied weakly.

I didn't want to tire her out even more by talking and talking. So I asked her permission to end my visit for the day. Then I would be with her again in the early morning. She was not aware of this yet because she was half asleep.

I then went to the hotel where I was going to spend the night. I wanted to go to bed early to be fresh in the morning and that's exactly what I did. The next morning I found her with a nurse sitting her on the edge of the bed. Today I had seen Nurgül in better condition. Of course, she was not in full health, but I hoped that in time she would recover. Today I would be able to spend the whole day with Nurgül, I just wanted to be with her. Yes, I just wanted to be with her now.

She could barely lean, or rather, she couldn't even lean on her bed while standing. Within a minute or two, the nurses entered the room to put her back to bed.

After a short conversation, she fell asleep. She was still in pain; she had had a difficult operation. The cables of several machines and the infusions were still connected. She must have lost a lot of blood, she was getting blood transfusions. I sat on a chair by the window, in the back, not visible from Nurgül's bed, who had been asleep for about an hour. Nurgül began to delirious in her sleep but she could not turn left or right, she could not even lift her head to look up. I listened to her crying from my seat. Slowly I got up from my chair, her face was turned to the wall, she was crying softly, "Papa, Papa ..." Nurgül had always left me alone when I cried, so I did too.

She would have a warm and trustworthy attitude like, *"Cry, my dear, be free and relaxed."* When I thought *that it would be one thing if I approached her bed and another if I did not,* she stopped crying and went back to sleep. It meant that she had lost her father, too. I had not known that until then.

Yes, we all lived our own destiny in one way or another. May God give us ease, endurance, patience, strength and fortitude in every trial He put us through. May God make his place heavenly.

Within half an hour, she woke up in pain. Unable to move from her seat, she tried to reach the button with one hand to call one of the nurses. The last nurse placed it so high that of course she could not reach it. Immediately I had gotten up and intervened, even though she was writhing in pain when she saw me, she said, "Yasemin, welcome. I'm trying to reach the button but I can't grasp it." "The nurses will be here soon," I replied, pressing the button as I walked from the other empty bed to her bed.

Since she had forgotten that I had come in the morning, she greeted me again. It must still be the effect of the anesthesia. "You should take this machine off me, I can't feel my right side at all, neither my leg nor my arm. I feel paralyzed," she breathed with weakness and pain. When the nurse came in, I had told her the same thing. "Have the anesthesiologist take it off, the other machine will also be taken off today. We are still giving anesthesia. It's easy to say remove it, do you know what the patient went through?" the nurse snapped at me.

Right, it was easy for me to say, I didn't know what the patient had been through. I felt very bad, took my jacket without saying anything and went downstairs to the cafeteria. How could I have known, I was not there for her.

I had quit smoking nine years ago but that day at that moment I had a strong craving for a cigarette. So I approached the smokers and asked, "Can you sell me a cigarette?" One of the young men immediately handed me a cigarette from his pack. As soon as I lit it, I felt dizzy and had to cough. But I was stubborn and took another drag. My blood pressure was zero. I then put it out and went back to the cafeteria. Oh my God, what an epidemic this was. I had smoked the stuff before and was glad I had quit. Many times Nurgül had said to me, "Yasemin, I feel sorry for you! You don't even know how to take a puff, give it up, stop smoking." I never forget that and I was able to stop because she had said it then and encouraged me. Before we had moved to the new city, I had quit.

When I got back to the room, they had changed her, removed the blood bag and the machine. Once again, she had fallen asleep. I think today will be like that all day. But I was with her, that was all that mattered. At prayer times, I went to my car and Nurgül prayed even though she couldn't move in her bed. My Almighty Lord, who gave the problem, also gives the solution, it seems, without a doubt.

Such a rhythm existed until the evening hours. After the device was removed, she started to feel better. Her right side began to feel something again and she could move her hand. When she spoke, she smiled from time to time.

Around four in the morning I wanted to leave, another long journey was ahead of me. That evening we had said goodbye but I wanted to come back.

On the same day, I was still at work without having been home before. In the evening I had spoken with Kiraz. On the phone she said to me that she wanted to come with me next time. We had a lot to talk about and a lot of problems had built up in Kiraz. So we could talk about the issues on the way.

When the weekend came and Kiraz and I were out, she told me that she had started writing applications for a job in Türkiye. My brother kept telling her that she should open her own business. He was right and I agreed with him. Somehow we had managed to convince Kiraz. She could realize her dream whether she started her own business or not. After she applied for a job as an interpreter at the Prime Minister's Office in Ankara, she was offered an interview by the ministry.

"I couldn't take the appointment they sent me and rescheduled it because it didn't coincide with my vacation," she explained.

"Don't be ridiculous!", I suddenly interrupted her.

"What postponement? The Prime Minister's Office gives you an appointment for an interview and you postpone it. What nonsense! You postponed it anyway, we can't change it,"

I replied, although I was actually nervous, I was very happy for Kiraz. I hoped that my sister would become an interpreter in the Prime Minister's office in Ankara, what an honorable feeling.

The drive took almost another two hours, Kiraz and I had considered returning to Türkiye for good and we still had six months to sort everything out. After that, we wanted to draw a line in Germany and make a new start in our own homeland.

When we arrived at the hospital to visit Nurgül, we entered the room and said, "What are we looking at?" She had gotten up and was walking around the room by herself. I was very happy to see this development. Of course, she was still in pain and holding on but that was okay. This was also progress, day by day she would get better and better.

That day we were able to spend a long time together. In the evening, when the streets were a little quieter, we wanted to go back with Kiraz. When she saw Kiraz, she said, "Yesterday she was up to my waist, today she is over my head. The years fly by, Yasemin." I told her about our return to Türkiye and she was happy. "It is logical and I hope this is the best and right decision for you," she replied.

And when she saw me with my head covered, she experienced a completely different honor and happiness. Yes, I was now covered. When we met, neither she nor I had spoken a single sentence about the cassettes I had sent and their contents.

It was evening, we said goodbye to her and I went back home with my Kiraz. Nurgül said she would stay at the hospital for a while. We promised to come back and so we said goodbye.

After an hour or two of driving, Kiraz fell asleep quietly in the car. An hour before we got home, she woke up again. I had taken a nap in the hospital room so I hadn't slept much.

We had reached our home safely. As soon as Kiraz arrived, she prepared for sleep and went to bed without wasting much time. A thousand and one things went through my mind again. Again, a new stage was waiting for us. Again a new life, a new line was approaching. In the meantime I had reached the end of my cassette again. But tonight I had talked a lot again. I hoped we would see each other again in my next cassette, goodbye ...

People polluted the black.
Whereas black;

it was peace, it was night, it was calm...

Yasemin's Struggle

CHAPTER
33

Yes, this is my last recording.

I had recorded my last cassette five months ago. We had been so busy lately that it was incredible but we had finally reached the end.

Kiraz was preparing for her final exams. She had to take three more exams, after which, God willing, my sister would graduate from university as an interpreter. In the meantime, I had handed over the second salon and soon I would hand over the house and the last hair salon. As for the house and the salon ... When Nurgül came out of the hospital, I told her that I wanted to give her both the house and the hair salon. She refused. When some time had passed again, I went to see her again one weekend. I asked her again face to face, I wanted her to accept and accept. But she insisted, "I will not accept and I will not accept". After I asked her why, she said, "My siblings are close to me, I have no intention of changing cities again. I am satisfied with my job as well as my personal life." I had to accept her decision, even though I didn't want to.

During these five months, we four brothers and sisters had been able to visit the Umrah. Our Lord had allowed us to enter the Holy Land. Each time we traveled to Türkiye, we took a little of our belongings with us.

At the urging of my brother and me, Kiraz needed an office in Türkiye and she had given her approval at the last minute. My brother had Kiraz's business cards and logo prepared for her new interpreting office and began promoting it. Kiraz was also hired as an interpreter at the Prime Ministry in Ankara.

Suat, on the other hand, put his head together with my brother Nihat. Now the two brothers were running the holding company. During her last visit to Türkiye, we had taken my aunt to private hospitals and doctors. From now on, her treatment would take place in Türkiye.

Through my brother, I had met a real estate agent to help me find a house. The real estate agent sent me information by e-mail but there were no favorites among them yet.

I was in no hurry, perhaps I should give up the hairdressing business altogether and retire to solitude as if I had been purified. With my hard-earned money I could build a house and a business from scratch. I had also started thinking about orphanages for orphans and institutions for people in need. From now on, I would definitely focus on these things.

Tobias and Steffi had gotten married and got used to life in Türkiye. They kept saying it was a country like paradise. They still praised Türkiye with great love, I was happy.

I had achieved many things, I no longer harbored feelings of revenge on anyone. Now I had taken revenge on them, one after the other, legally, as it was proper! From now on, no one could harm me.

By the way, thanks to my lawyer, bloody Nigar, Kiraz was able to visit her own mother in prison. She was looking for her mother's wings, her arm, her smell. But she did not expect to meet such a person. She came back full of disappointment. Suat didn't want her to go at first, he tried to persuade Kiraz not to go but it was in vain. Finally, Kiraz had to go through this experience herself. When she came back from Türkiye, she said to me, "You are both my mother and my father" How painful that was but without a doubt, my Lord who gave the problem also gives the cure.

Yes, we had reached the end. You see. From where to where? This is actually an exemplary life story; I had drawn a clean line under my past, I could not erase everything negative I had experienced. Why was that? It had happened. It had nested inside me like a naughty guest but I was able to prevail with my determination and fighting spirit.

Let me briefly mention why Nurgül was very different for me.

Because she was the one who had embraced me in the first days without even knowing me, she was the first one who had said, "Speak, Yasemin!" She was the one who had tirelessly written my story. Although she was down and tired, she trusted me and did not give up. Yes, I had found my peace as I spoke. Day by day my wounds diminished, day by day my burden became lighter.

We had three weeks left in Germany. After three weeks, we wanted to leave Germany and we wanted to draw a line here.

Tomorrow was Saturday and I would like to present my last cassette to Nurgül personally. Nurgül had already recovered and started working after a long period of illness. Even though it was difficult, life went on. We had set the date for our meeting weeks ago. I absolutely accept that there would be a lack of something here and there.

It was my last recording, I was very quiet. Around me it smelled like goodbye. I didn't like these separations at all ... This goodbye was one of the things I could not get used to ...

Yasemin's despair and Yasemin's struggle had been published and put on the market. My life story had been rewritten. Tomorrow I was going to request a signed book from Nurgül. I was very excited and the book my revenge would be published soon without much time passing.

We had reached the end of my true life story An exemplary tale of life for some.

Look: On the cover of the book of Yasemin's Struggle, Nurgül has written as a subtitle, it in a collective sense as "the voice of one Yasemin among thousands of Yasemins". Yes. "I" was just the voice of one Yasemin among thousands of Yasemins! We have many more Yasemins whose voices are not heard and whose voices were trapped. They still suffered persecution, torture, violence, incest, rape, fear and victimization. Do not silence Yasemin's voice. Hear the voices of Yasemins who have suffered. Hear our voices and make them heard ....

Goodbye!

I took a deep breath and reached the end of my work entitled "Yasemin's Revenge". Yasemin personally handed me the fifteenth cassette and her last cassette at our last meeting. We were able to spend a very nice day together that day. I didn't know yet what she had recorded on the last two cassettes. But I was going to find out when I started working on them. I could tell that I had all kinds of experiences in those works.

It was a fact that Yasemin's true life story, which began sad and sorrowful, had come to such a beautiful end. It had made me very relieved and happy. I think she had finished it with a beautiful ending. Therefore, without further ado, I am ending my notes in a peaceful way because the life story I had written ended in itself.

I hoped that it will be a strength for all Yasemins. I wished each of them strength, fortitude, perseverance and patience in my heart. I wish that those who commit oppression will be punished as soon as possible.

You are not alone!

Together we are strong!

Silence!
If you shut up, you lose!

The End

READER COMMENTS

Hello, dear Mrs. Nurgül. It›s been a week since I read your books. Believe me, I can›t get rid of the effect. What happened is very painful. But I also congratulated Yasemin for being such a strong woman. In life, it is important not to give up. Blessings to your pen, your heart. May your success continue.

Fatoş TOPAL

As soon as I finished the first and second books, I immediately picked up the third. I began reading Yasemin›s Revenge with curiosity and excitement. I think I, like Yasemin, will be relieved in every line I read. I picked up the book hoping to read the lines where the wicked are seen as punished and victims are seen as just. I hope Yasemin is very happy now. Blessings to your pen, your heart, your love.

ESMDKC

Ms. Nurgül, I have read many comments about your books and have bought and read your books in confidence. I really congratulate you. I can say that it is burned in my memory. You have reflected very well what is happening today. I also congratulate Yasemin. May your pen last forever and your path be clear.

ANONYM

I came across this book series everywhere. I was very interested in the name of the book and finally decided to read it. When I started reading your book, I came across a simple colloquial language. We were almost us: you, Yasemin and me. Your sincere expression and language drew me into the book and the subject. The desired message reaches the reader. I congratulate you on your books of the Yasemin series, which I can only recommend and wish you much success.

ANONYM

Hello everyone. Let me get straight to the point: Your works should definitely be read and taught. When real experiences are written down so clearly, it shows that there are more lessons that people and humanity need to learn. Unfortunately, the problems mentioned in your book are very common today. Fortunately, there are authors like you, and such works are being written. Maybe someone will read them and be ashamed of them. With love and respect.

Ethem Namık KARAKUŞ

Nurgül, we met you at the fair. When I bought your book, I read it as soon as I got home. I am glad that I read it. I feel more confident now. At least it teaches us not to give up and strive. Not to mention the other Chapters. Don't stop writing. I love you very much.

Rümeysa KOVA

Hello... Health to your hands, heart, pen. I kiss your compassionate, conscientious heart full of love. After you read and finish the book, here is the real world book for you, a real life story. Is there any more? No, of course there isn›t. I will talk to my theatre team and tell our audience about your book during our performance. We will not be silent either, I will do my best, we will not silence Yasemin›s voice, just like you. We owe it to the Yasemins to contribute. I wish you continued success, goodbye.

Sevilay TURAN

Hi! This series book is a real life story. When I started reading I began to wonder, after a while the book drew me in. You turn one page at a time and wait curiously for the next. I read it without getting bored and finished in no time. Pure suspense. I highly recommend it to friends who are looking for other books. You will not regret it.
Love, greetings.

ANONYM

I liked the books very much, I couldn›t put them down and you can understand that I read them through in four days. I would love to have my books signed when you come to Mersin. I will also follow your next books and wish you continue success in your work.

Nermin KESKİN

Dear Ms. Sönmez ...
I am very glad that I found you. I finished your book series in two days,
an exemplary life story. Yasemin suffered a lot, may God reward her.
Who knows how you felt when you heard this story of Yasemin. It must
have been a very difficult job for you. Blessings to your hand and pen,
best regards.

ANONYM

Hello Ms. Nurgül. I hope that your books will reach many
people, because such works should be read and spread. Today›s events are
all about these issues. It is really a great success that you dare and write
something like this.

ANONYM

Hello dear Nurgül. It was the most impressive and meaningful
painful life story I have ever read. Officially, it was the first and only
book that hurt me from my bones to my soul, my throat felt like it was
tightening. I am also an orphan and a full orphan at that. I live with my
brothers so I could find and take on what my namesake went through.
God willing, one day we will all find peace. It is a very difficult test. I,
too, have greatly appreciated your life and work. You never lost your faith
and love for God. May your success continue, dear Nurgül. It is good
that there are people like you.

ANONYM

Matilda Türkçe

Savaşın İçinden Bir Kelebek

Sert Kapak - İnce Kapak - e-kitap

Matilda Deutsch

Ein Schmetterling inmitten des Krieges

Paperback - Hardcover - e-book

Matilda English

A butterfly through the war

Paperback - Hardcover - e-book

Yasemin'in Çaresizliği - 1 Türkçe

Binlerce Yasemin'den Bir Yasemin'in Sesi

Sert Kapak - İnce Kapak - e-kitap

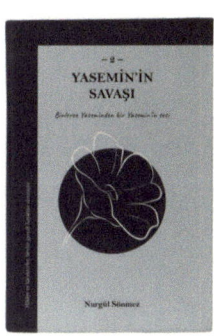 

Yasemin'in Savaşı - 2 Türkçe

Binlerce Yasemin'den Bir Yasemin'in Sesi

Sert Kapak - İnce Kapak - e-kitap

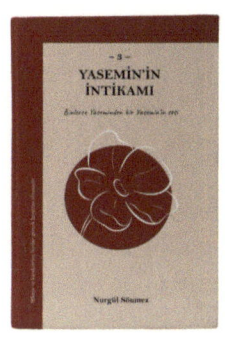 

Yasemin'in İntikamı - 3 Türkçe

Binlerce Yasemin'den Bir Yasemin'in Sesi

Sert Kapak - İnce Kapak - e-kitap

Yasemins Verzweiflung - 1 Deutsch

Eine Stimme unter Tausenden

Paperback - Hardcover - e-book

Yasemins Kampf - 2 Deutsch

Eine Stimme unter Tausenden

Paperback - Hardcover - e-book

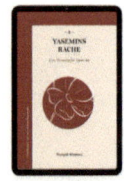

Yasemins Rache - 3 Deutsch

Eine Stimme unter Tausenden

Paperback - Hardcover - e-book

Yasemins Desperation - 1 English

One voice among thousands

Paperback - Hardcover - e-book

Yasemins Struggle - 2 English

One voice among thousands

Paperback - Hardcover - e-book

Yasemins Revenge - 3 English

One voice among thousands

Paperback - Hardcover - e-book

1001 Gece Yerine Bin Bir Gün Türkçe

"Özgürlüğe süzülen bir mülteci"

Sert Kapak - İnce Kapak - e-kitap

Statt 1001 Nacht - Tausendundein Tag Deutsch

"Weg in die Freiheit"

Paperback - Hardcover - e-book

Instead Of 1001 Night – One Thousand and One Day English

"A refugee soaring to freedom"

Paperback - Hardcover - e-book

Maarouf Türkçe

"Vatanı tarafından terk edilmiş bir adamın, inanılmaz öyküsü"

Sert Kapak - İnce Kapak - e-kitap

Maarouf Deutsch

"Ein Mann, der von seiner Heimat verlassen wurde"

Paperback - Hardcover - e-book

Maarouf English

"The incredible story of a man abandoned his homeland by force"

Paperback - Hardcover - e-book

Teklif ediyoruz:

Almanca, İngilizce, Fransızca ve Türkçe dillerinde
uzman edebi kitap çevirileri.

. *Editörlük*
- **Almanca, İngilizce, Fransızca, Türkçe**

. *Düzeltme*
- **Almanca, İngilizce, Fransızca, Türkçe**

Nous offrons :

Des traductions littéraires professionnelles
de livres en allemand, anglais, français et turc.

. *Lectorat*
- **Allemand, Anglais, Français, Turc**

. *Lecture de correction*
- **Allemand, Anglais, Français, Turc**

Eserlerinizden çevirmekle
ilgileniyor musunuz?
O zaman lütfen bize bir
e-posta gönderin.

MERHABA · HALLO · HELLO

f nurgulsonmez
✉ ns.nurgulsonmez@gmail.com
⊙ nurgulsonmezofficial

Nurgül Sönmez
– Schriftstellerin –

■ **Sunduğumuz hizmetler:**

Almanca, İngilizce, Fransızca ve Türkçe dillerinde uzman edebi kitap çevirileri.

• Editörlük - Almanca, İngilizce, Fransızca, Türkçe
• Düzeltme - Almanca, İngilizce, Fransızca, Türkçe

Siz de eser(ler)inizin çevirisini yapmak ve ek hizmetlerimizden (redaksiyon, düzenleme, kitap kapağı tasarımı, illüstrasyon & kitap dizgisi) yararlanmak istiyorsanız bize ulaşın.

➤ Talebinizi bize e-posta ile gönderebilirsiniz.

■ **Nous offrons:**

Des traductions littéraires professionnelle des livre en allemand, anglais, française et turc.

• Lectorat - Allemand, Anglais, Français, Turc
• Lecture de correction - Allemand, Anglais, Français, Turc

Vous êtes également intéressé par la traduction littéraire de votre ou vos œuvres et par le bénéfice de nos services complémentaires (relecture, correction, conception de couvertures de livres, illustration et composition de livres).

➤ Alors envoyez-nous votre demande par e-mail.

ns.nurgulsonmez@gmail.com

Wir bieten:

In den Sprachen **Deutsch, Englisch, Französisch & Türkisch** fachgerechte literarische Buchübersetzung an.

• Lektorat
- Deutsch, Türkisch, Englisch, Französisch
• Korrekturlesen
- Deutsch, Türkisch, Englisch, Französisch

Sie haben auch Interesse eines Ihrer Werke zu Übersetzen? Dann schreiben Sie uns gerne ein Email.

We offer:

Professional literary book translation in **German, English, French & Turkish.**

• Editing
- German, Turkish, English, French
• Proofreading
- German, Turkish, English, French

MERHABA
HALLO
HELLO

nurgulsonmez
ns.nurgulsonmez@gmail.com
nurgulsonmezofficial

Nurgul Sonmez
- Schriftstellerin -

■ **Wir bieten:**

In den Sprachen Deutsch, Englisch, Türkisch und Französisch fachgerechte literarische Buchübersetzung an. Zusätzlich;
• Lektorat - Deutsch, Englisch, Türkisch, Französisch
• Korrekturlesen - Deutsch, Englisch, Türkisch, Französisch

Sie haben auch Interesse Ihr Werk oder Ihre Werke literarisch zu Übersetzen und von unseren zusätzlichen Dienstleistungen zu profitieren (Lektorat, Korrekturlesen, Buchcover Design, Illustration & Buchsatz).

▷ Dann schicken Sie uns Ihre Anfrage per Email.

■ **We offer:**

Professional literary book translation in German, English, Turkish and French.
• Editing - German, English, Turkish, French
• Droofreading - German, English, Turkish, French

You are also interested in literary translation of your work(s) and benefit from our additional services (Editing, droofreading, book cover design, illustration & book typesetting).

▷ Then send us your request by email.